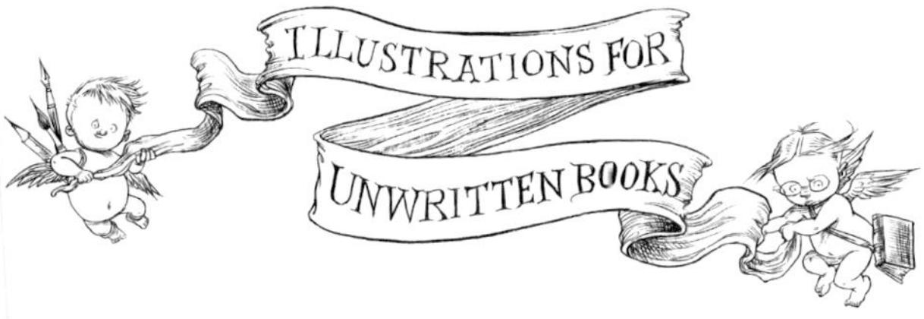
ILLUSTRATIONS FOR
UNWRITTEN BOOKS

Text and illustrations copyright © 2005 by Chris Riddell

First U.S. edition 2006

Library of Congress Cataloging-in-Publication Data is available.

Library of Congress Catalog Card Number pending

ISBN-10 0-7636-3053-5
ISBN-13 978-0-7636-3053-9

10 9 8 7 6 5 4 3 2 1

Printed in United States of America

This book was typeset in Goudy Hundred.
The illustrations were done in pen and ink.

Candlewick Press
2067 Massachusetts Avenue
Cambridge, Massachusetts 02140

visit us at www.candlewick.com

THE DA VINCI COD

AND OTHER ILLUSTRATIONS FOR UNWRITTEN BOOKS

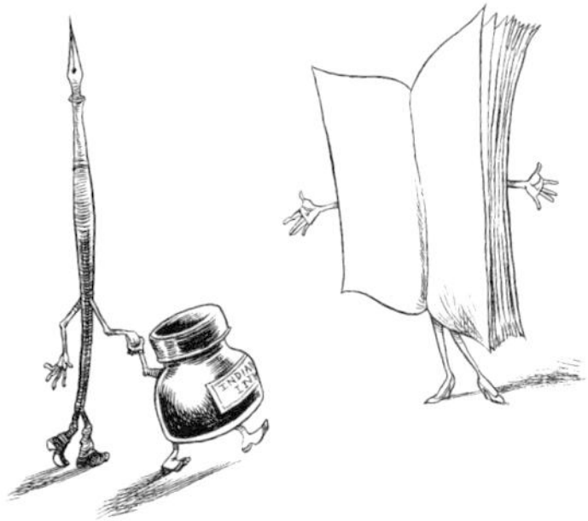
INDIAN INK

Chris Riddell

CANDLEWICK PRESS
CAMBRIDGE, MASSACHUSETTS

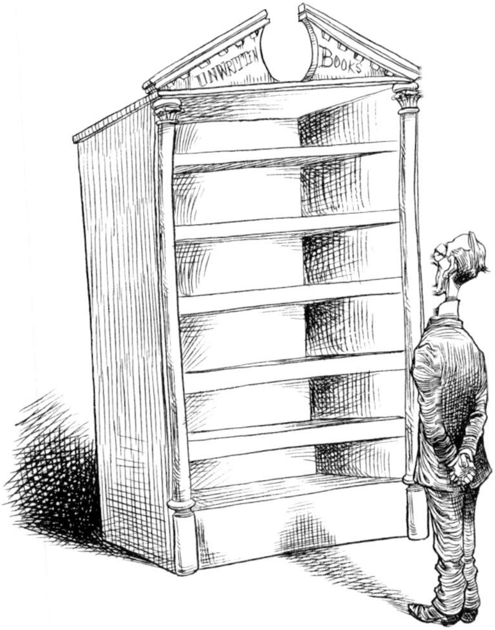
UNWRITTEN
BOOKS

FOR ALL AT

THE LITERARY REVIEW

Foreword

There are many shelves in the library of unwritten
books, all of them empty. Although this is a drawback
for the dedicated reader, it is a positive godsend for
the enterprising artist, as the number of unwritten books
is literally infinite and all of them require illustrations.
As the books are unwritten, there are no complicated
passages to wade through, no implausible plot twists,
no disappointing endings. They take up no space,
never get dog-eared, never smell like moldy underwear,
and are very reasonably priced. But the
greatest virtue of unwritten books from the point
of view of an illustrator is that they have no
authors — no authors to complain, interfere, and
pretend they know best. So here, for the first time,
collected into a slim volume, fragrantly priced
and easy on the eye are illustrations to some
of the finest books never written.

Chris Riddell

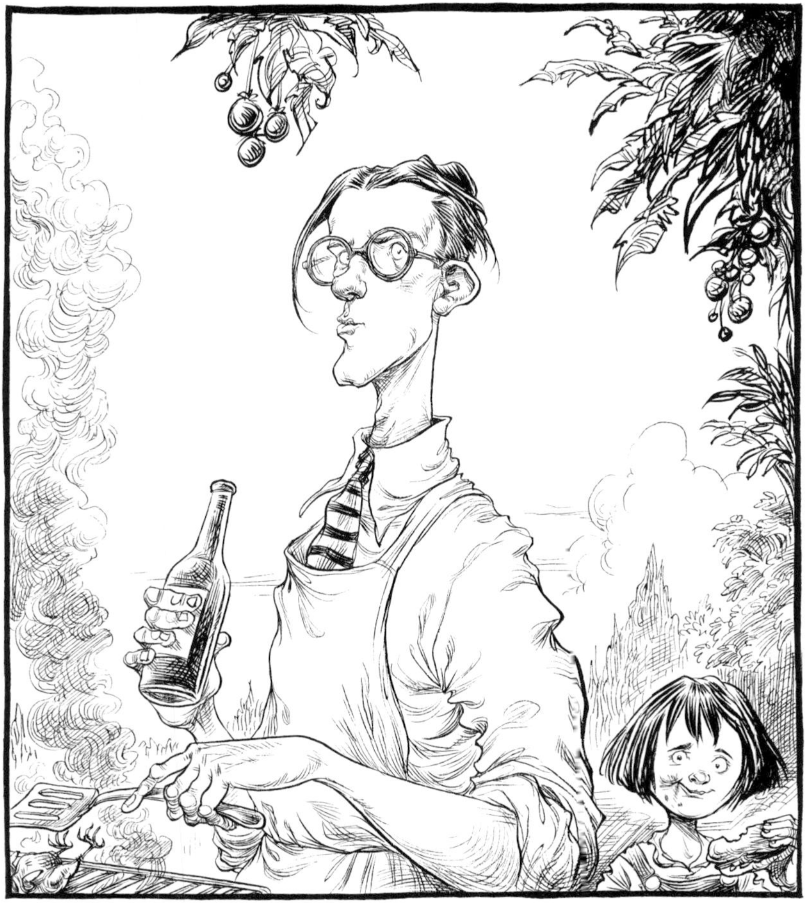

TO GRILL A MOCKINGBIRD

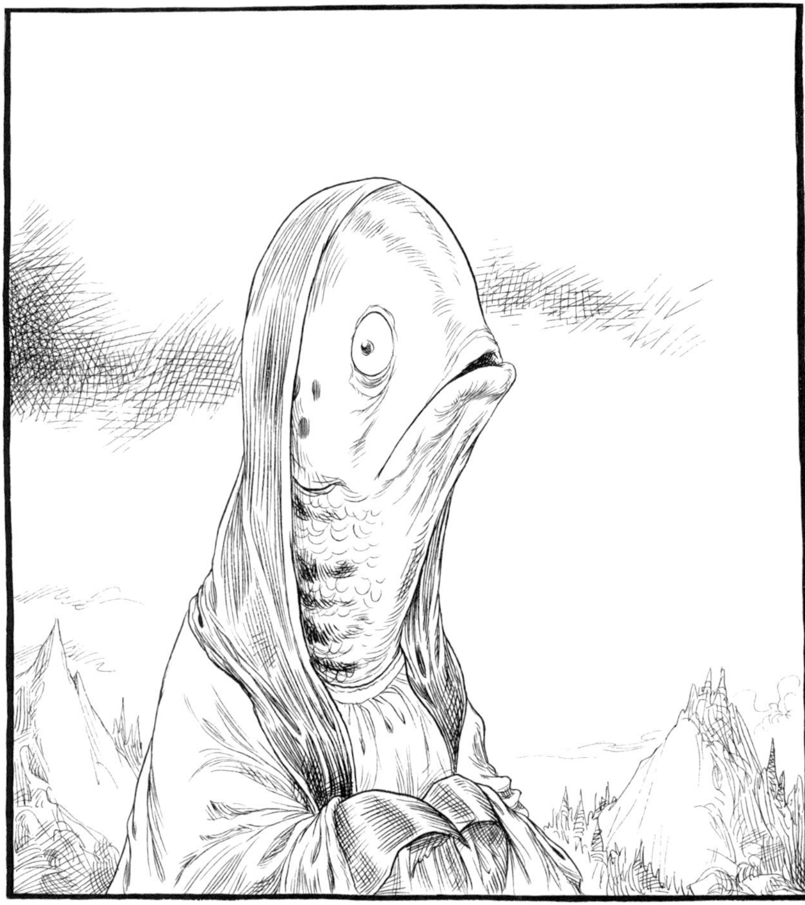

THE DA VINCI COD

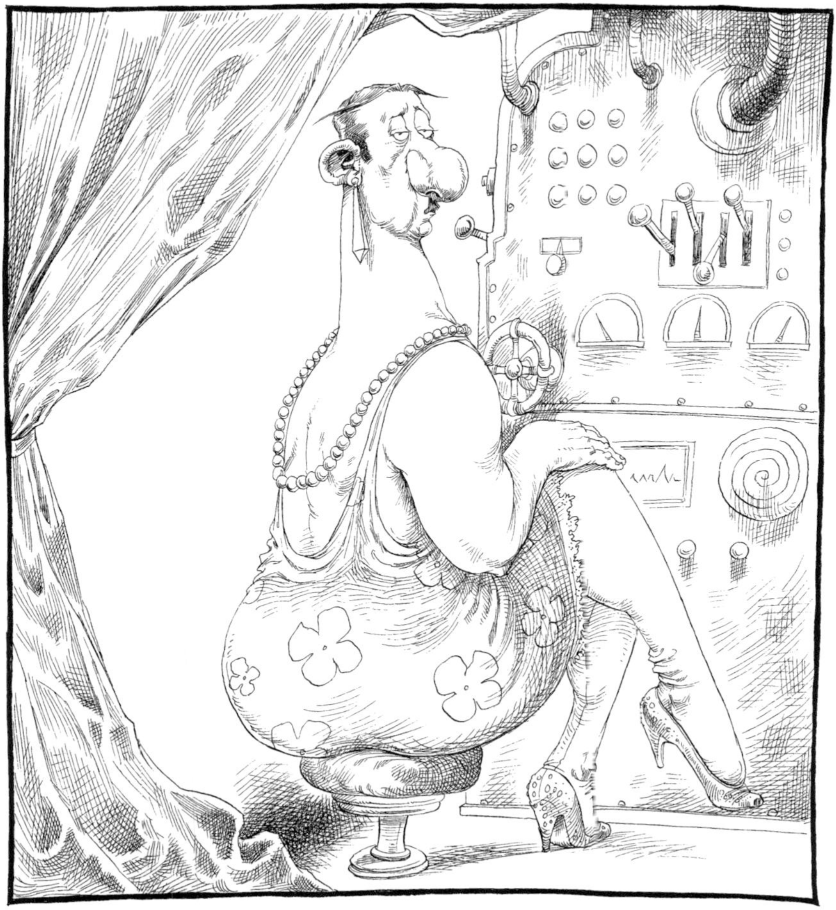

THE WIZARD OF ODD

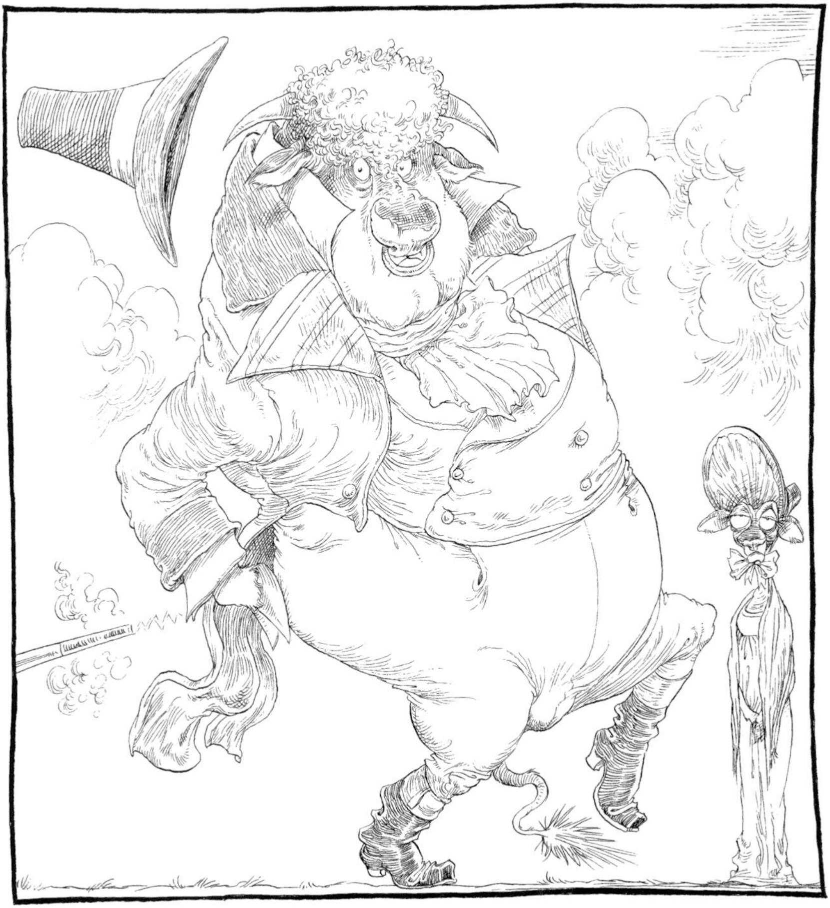

Prod and Prejudice

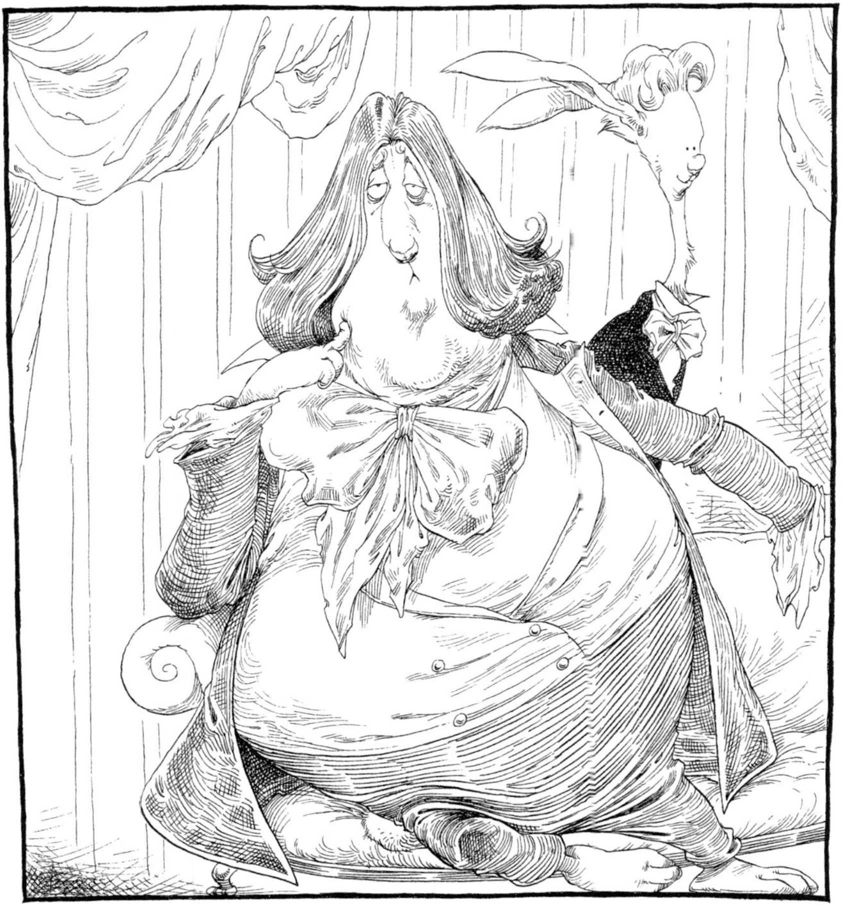

THE IMPORTANCE OF BEING EARLESS

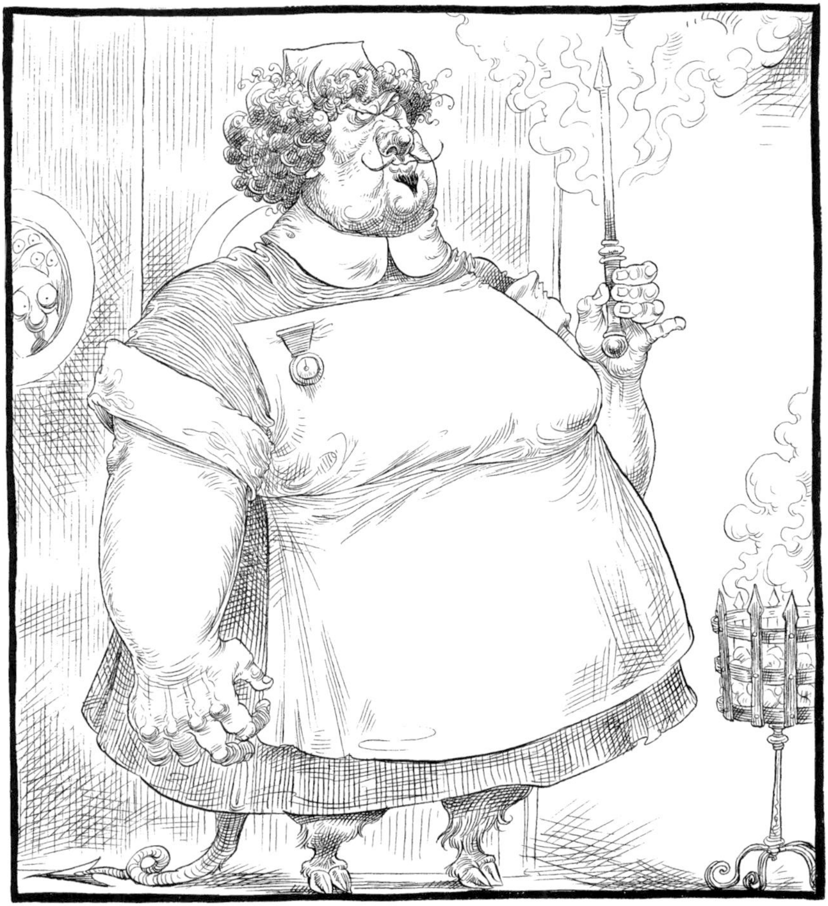

THE SATANIC NURSES

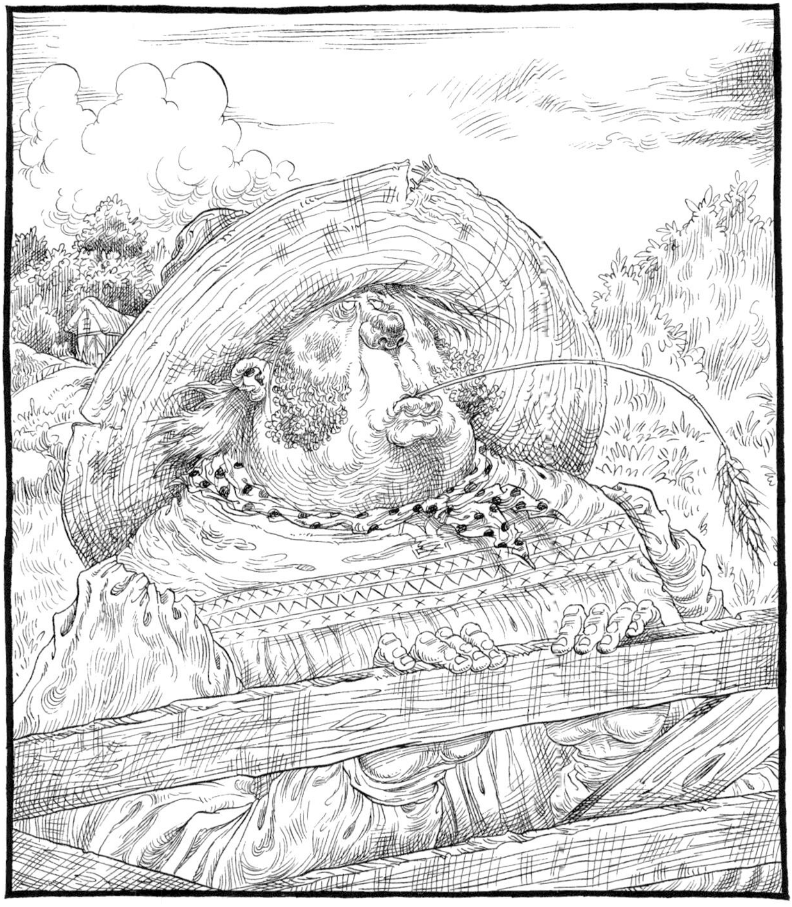

JUDE THE OBVIOUS

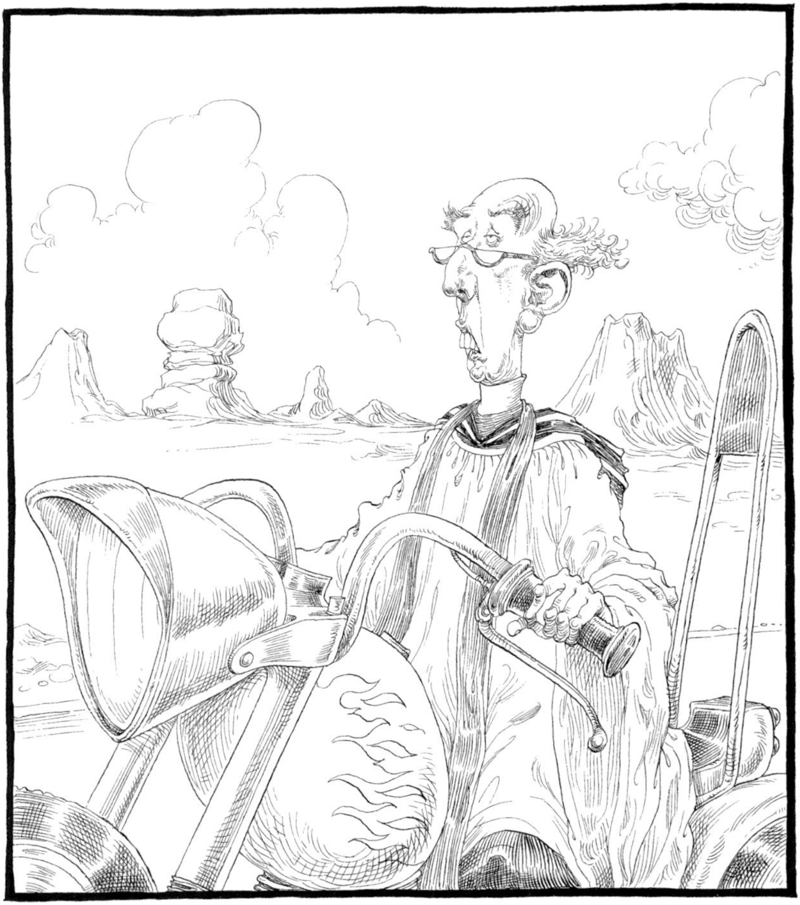

ANGLICANISM AND THE ART OF MOTORCYCLE MAINTENANCE

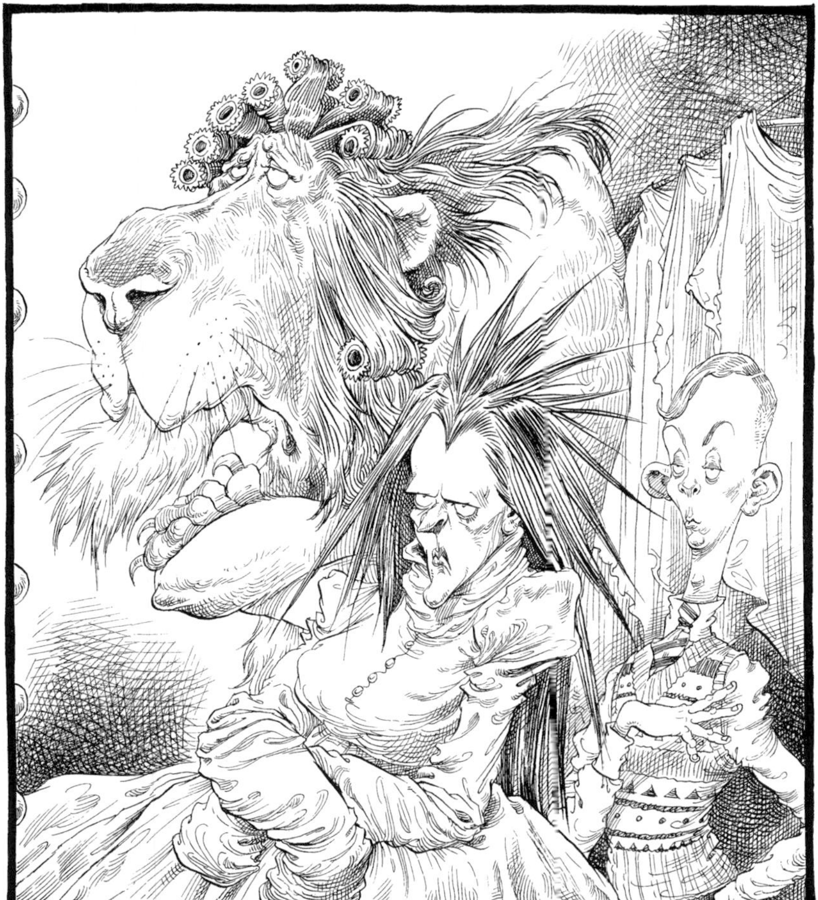

THE LION, THE WITCH AND THE WARDROBE ASSISTANT

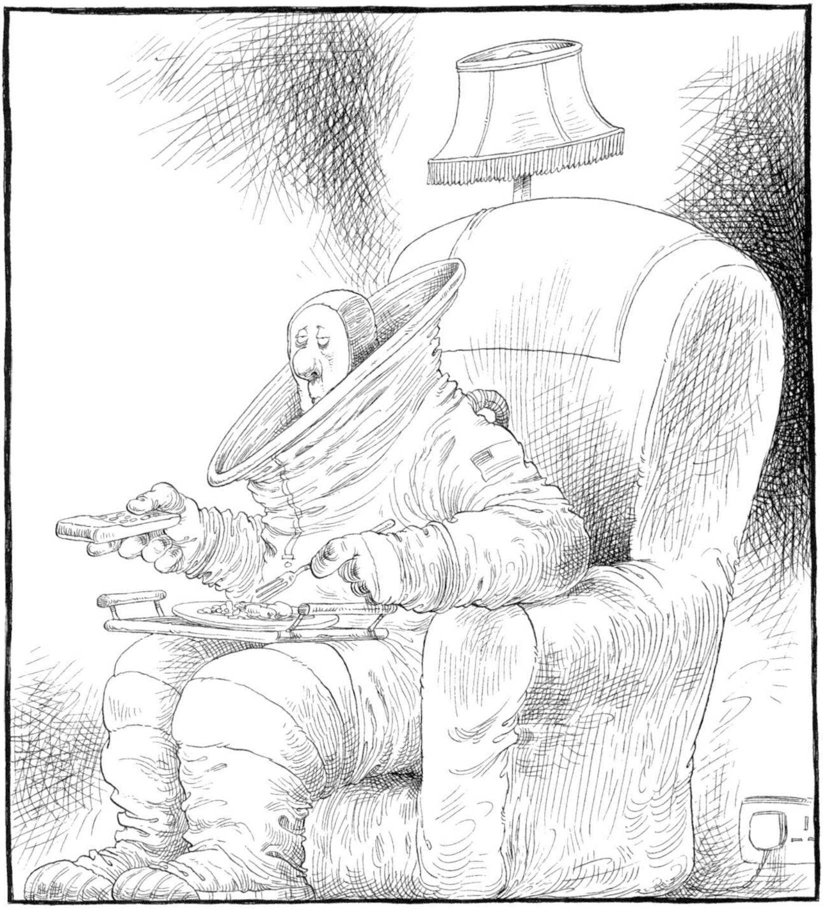

2001: A SPACE QUIET-NIGHT-IN

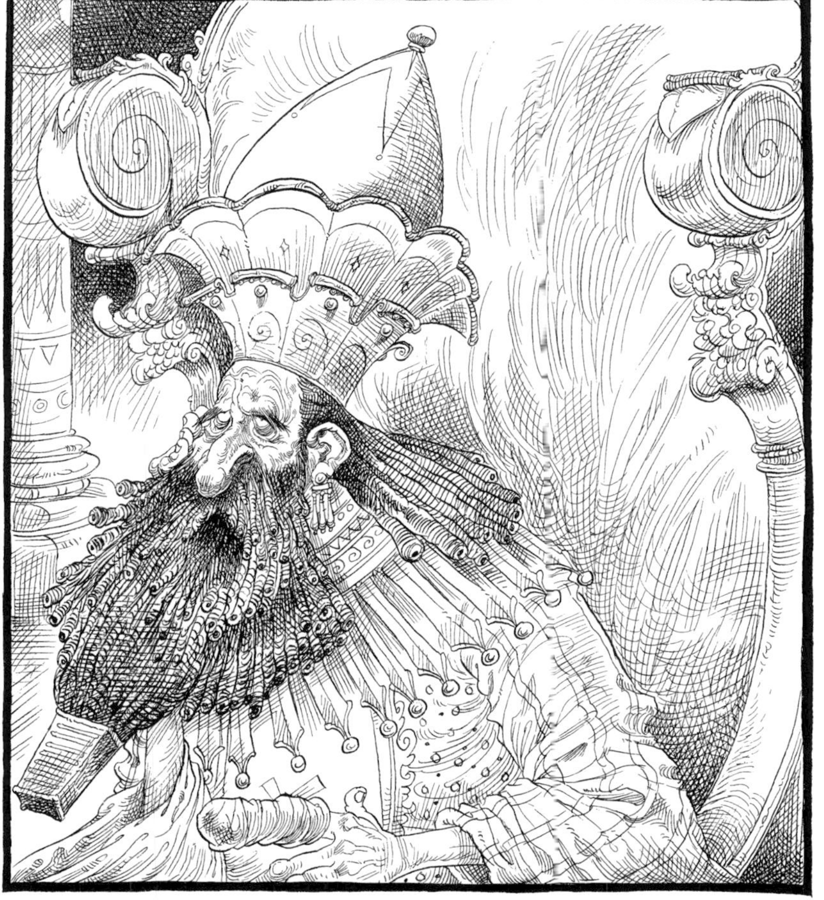

King Solomon's Moans

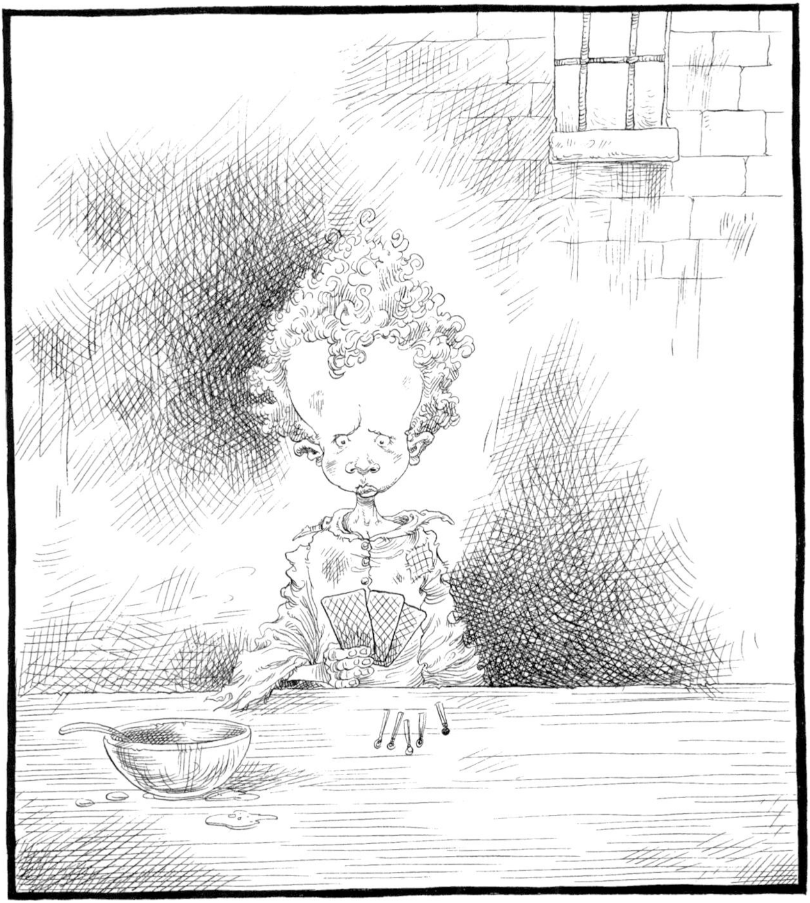

OLIVER BUST

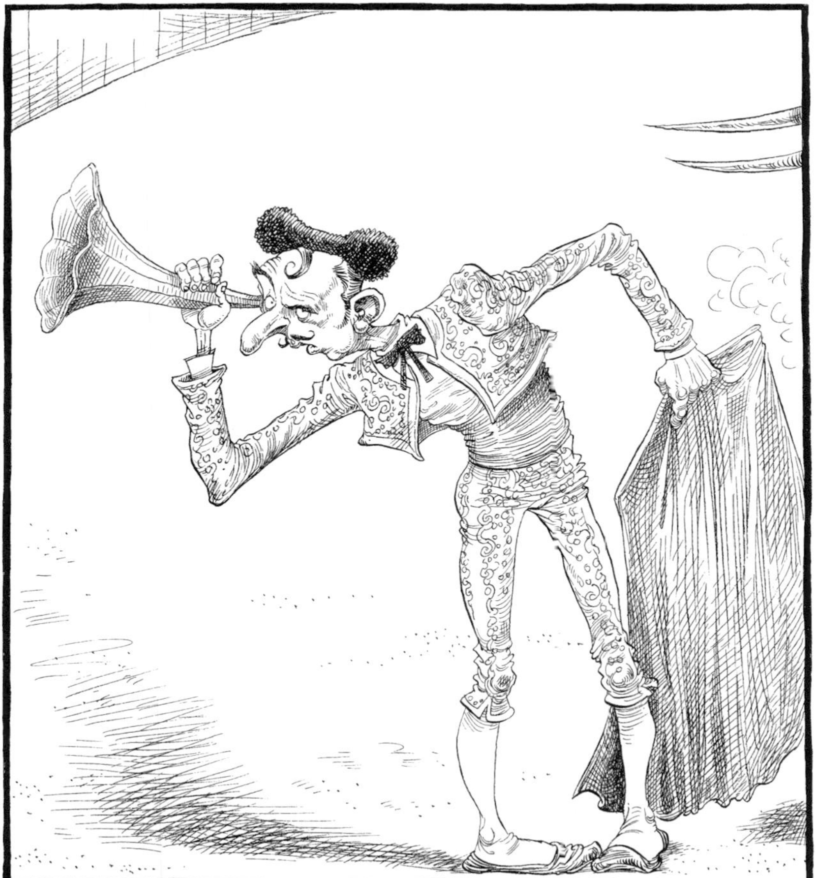

DEAF IN THE AFTERNOON

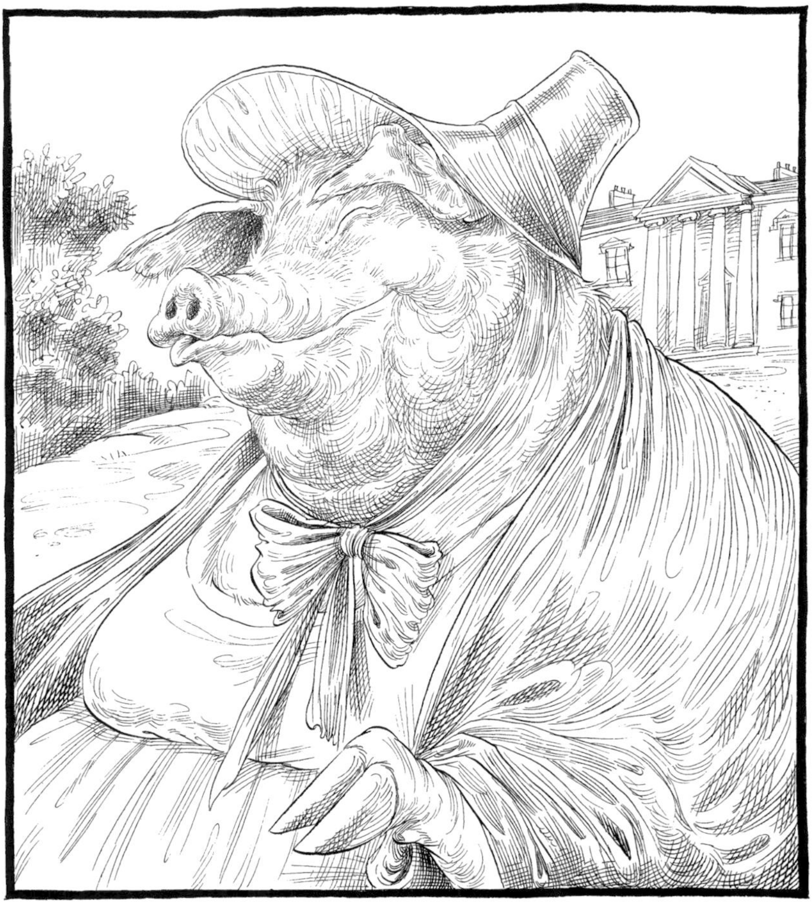

MANSFIELD PORK

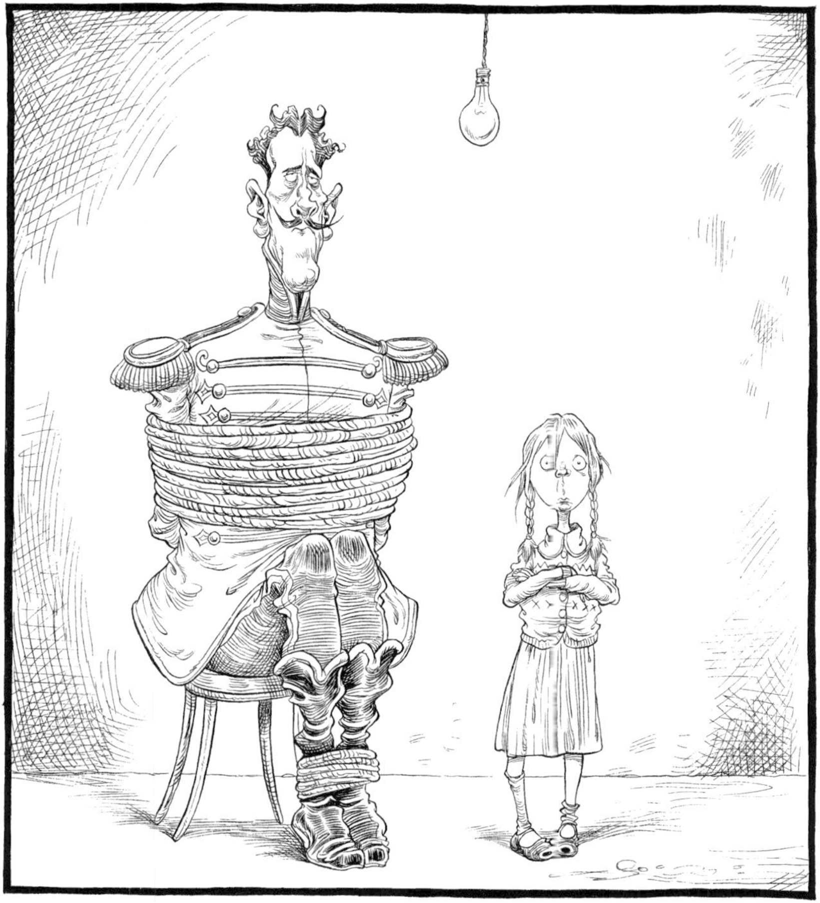

THE PRISONER OF BRENDA

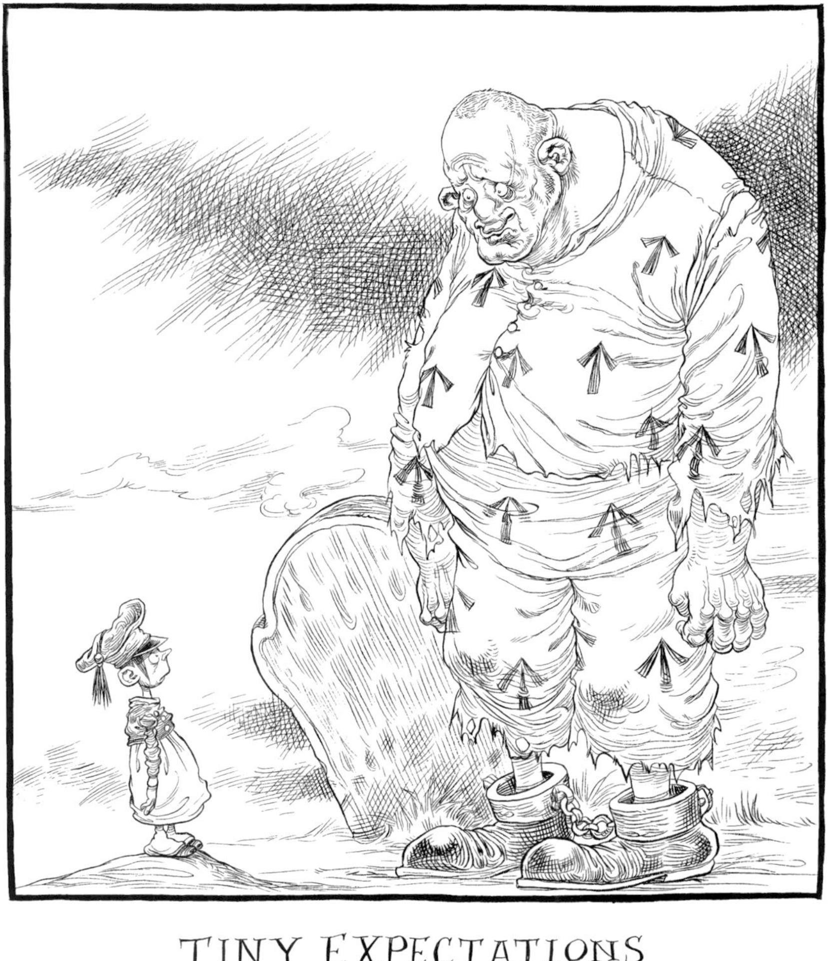

TINY EXPECTATIONS

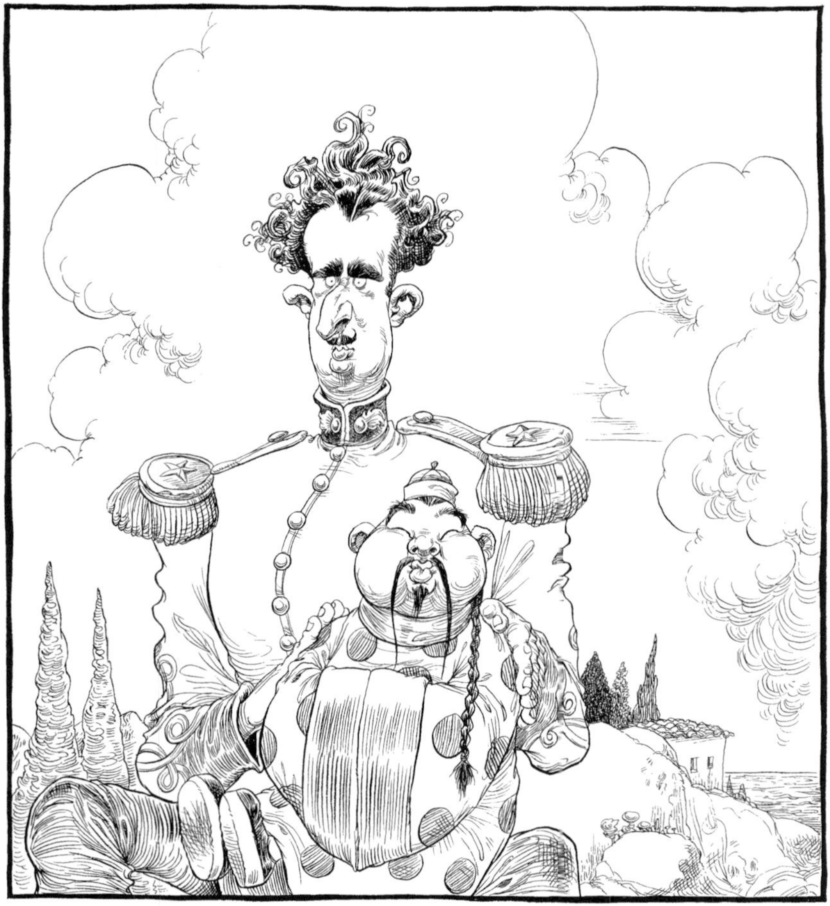

CAPTAIN CORELLI'S MANDARIN

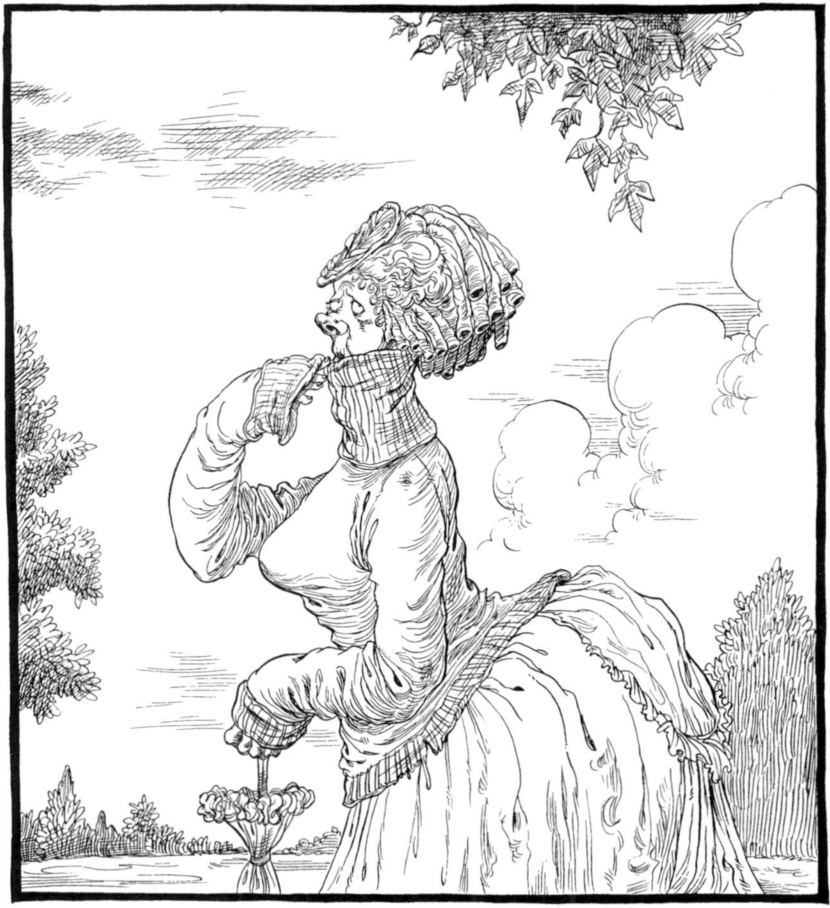

A WOOLLEN OF NO IMPORTANCE

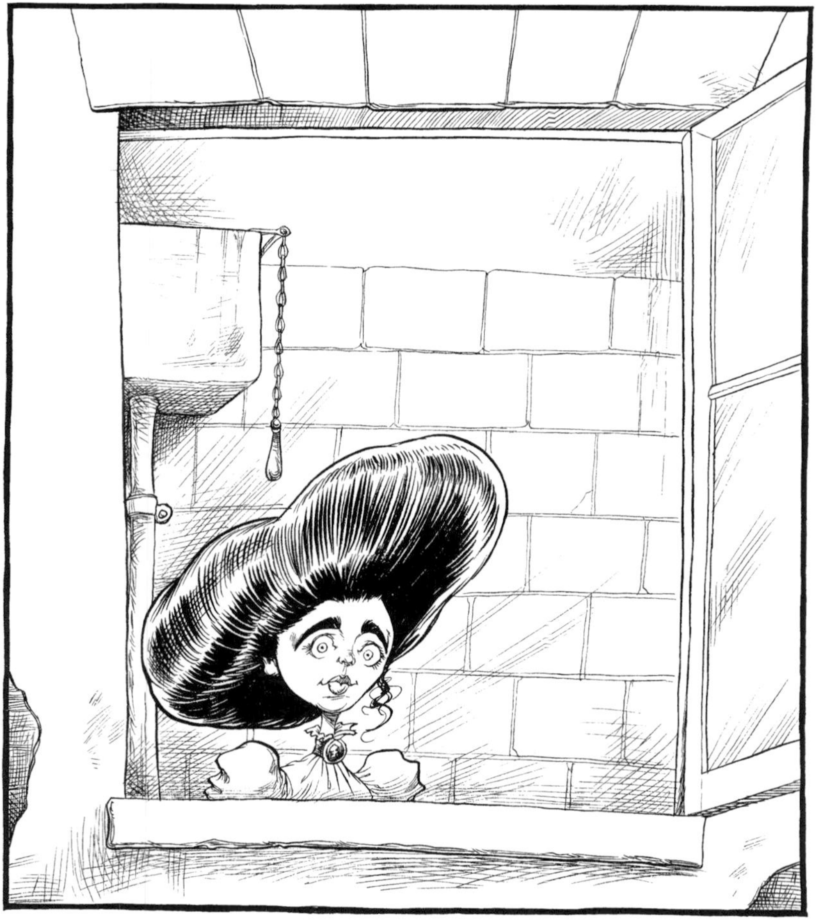

A Room with a Loo

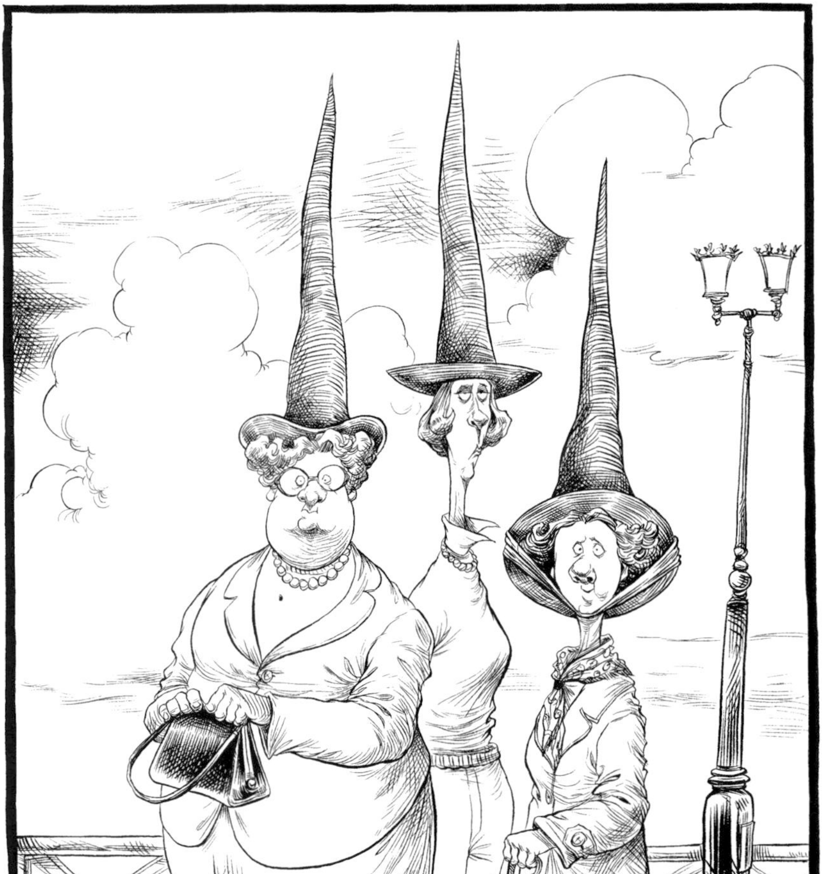

THE WITCHES OF EAST HAMPTON

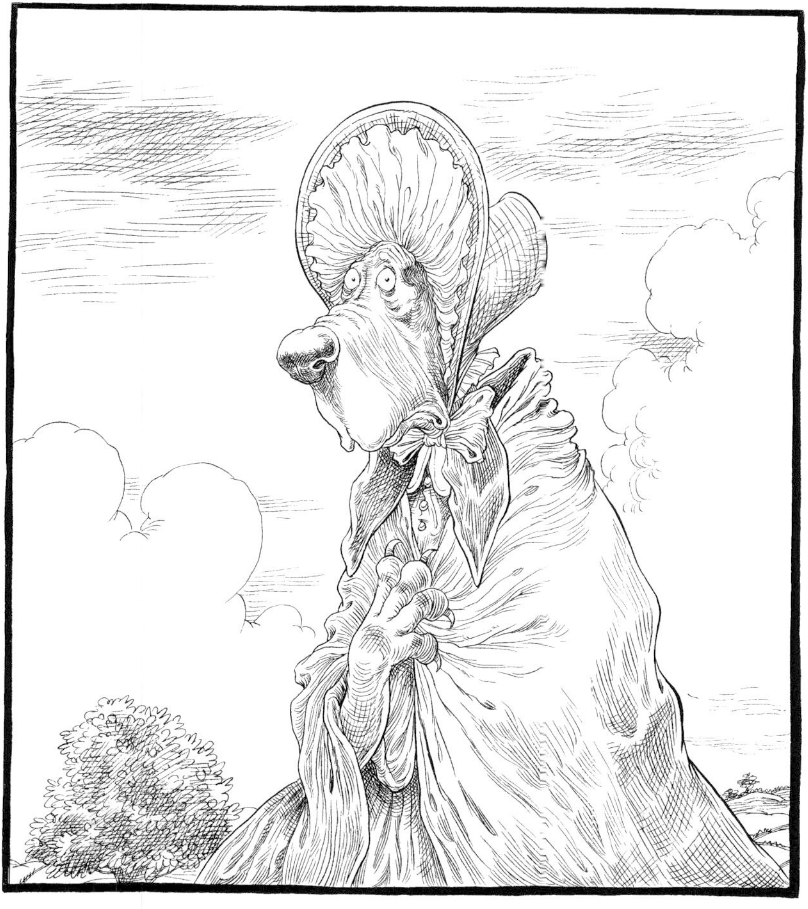

TESS OF THE BASKERVILLES

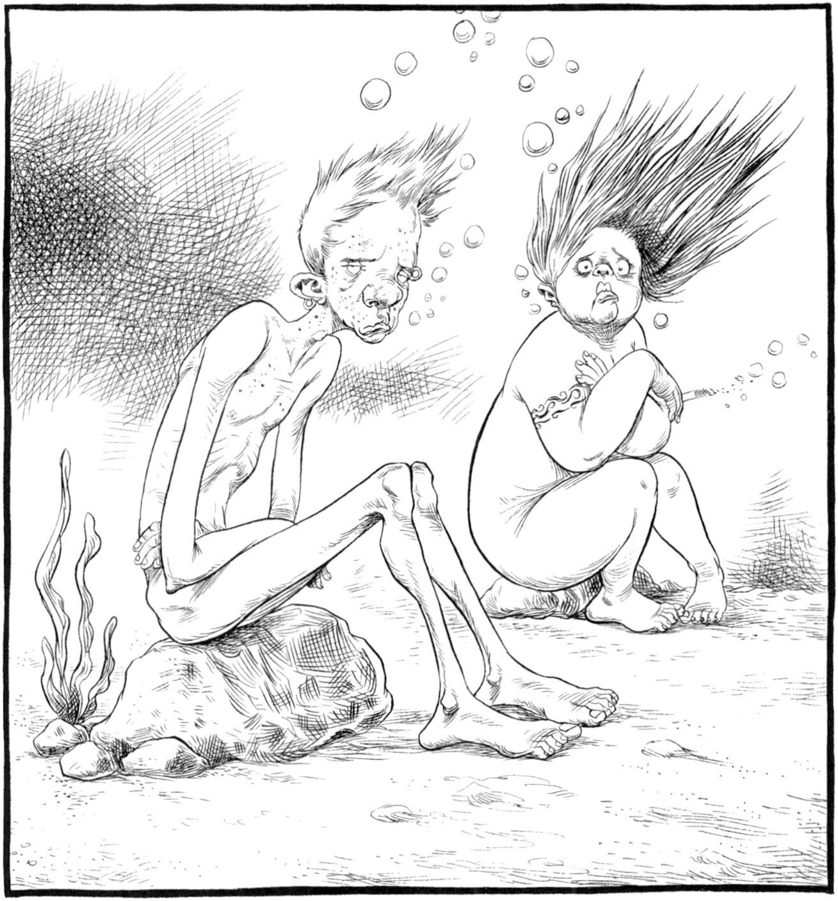

THE WATER ADOLESCENTS

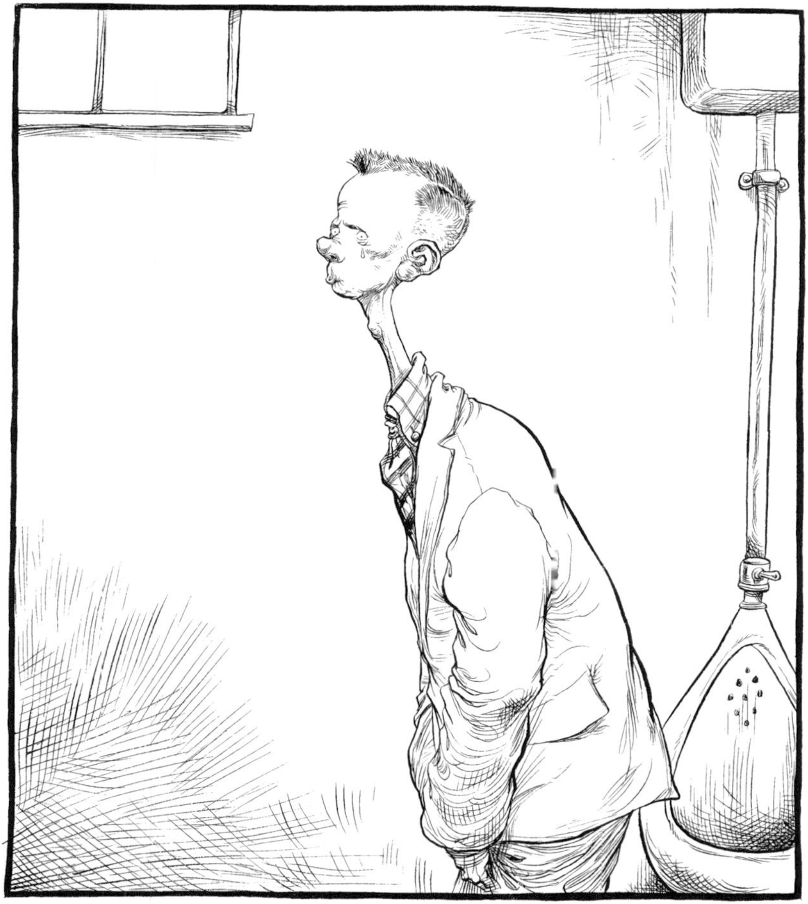

THE CATCHER IN THE FLY

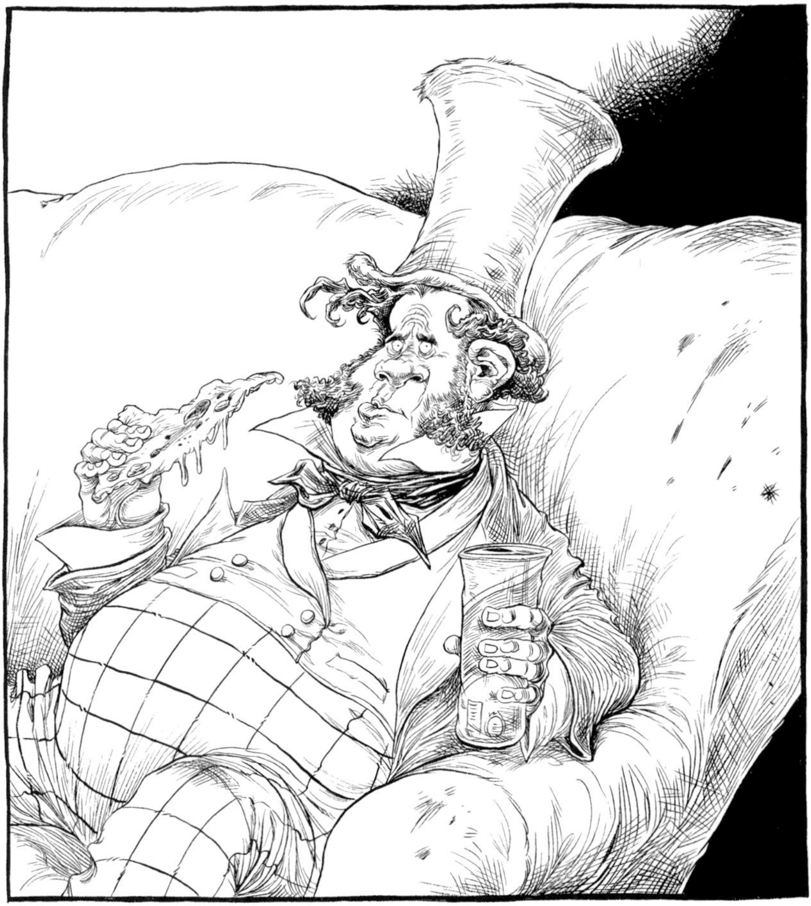

BLOKE HOUSE

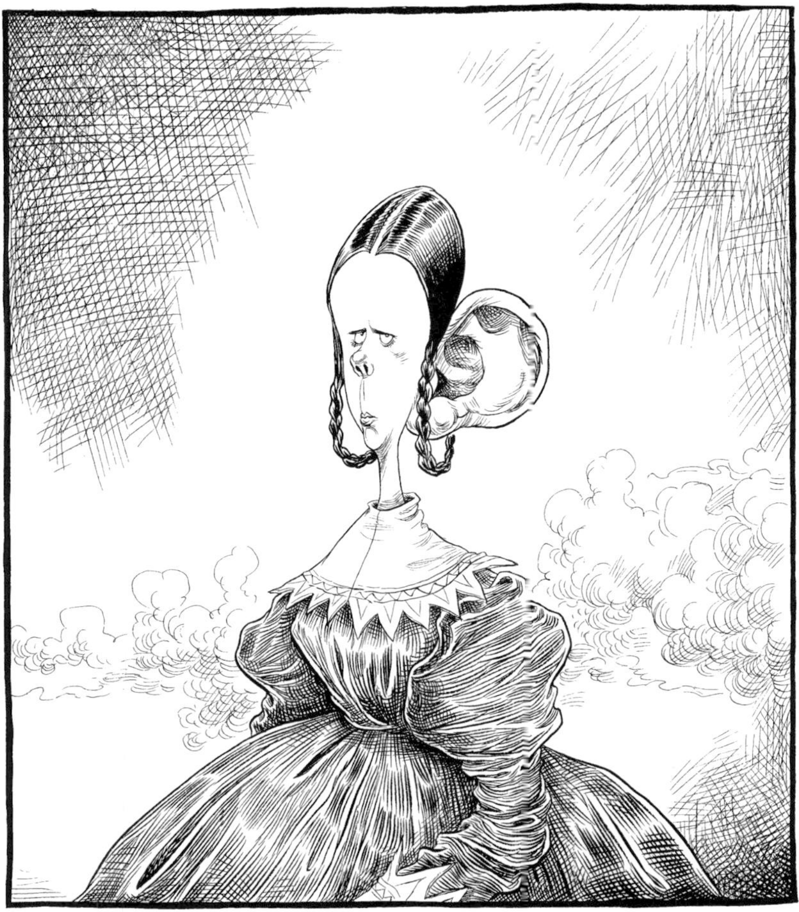

JANE EAR

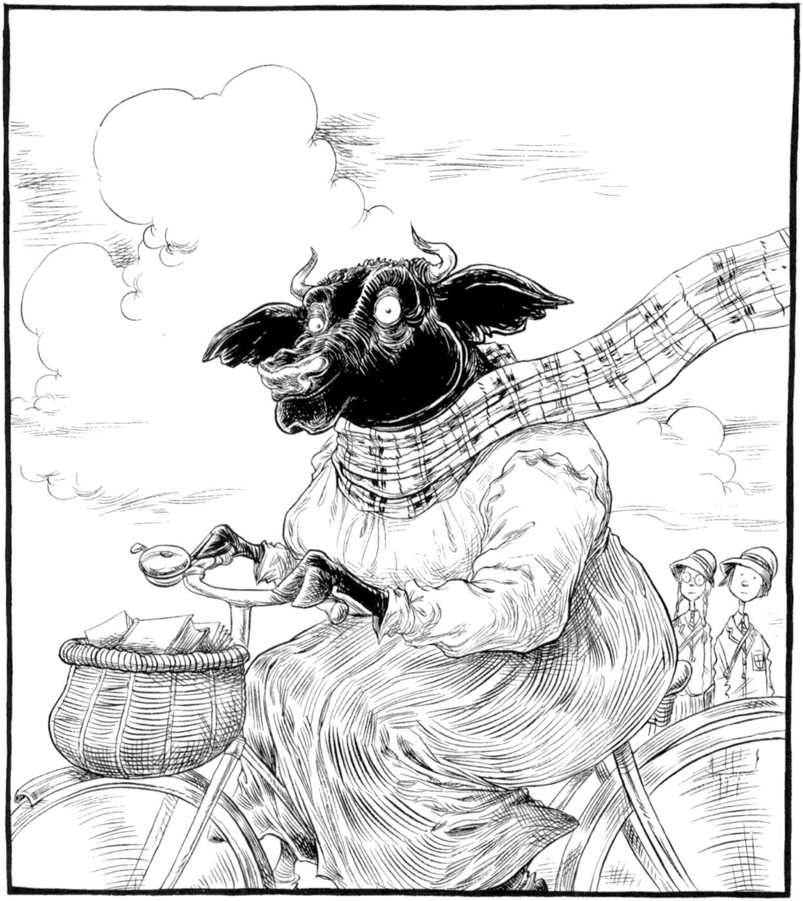

THE PRIME OF MISS ABERDEEN ANGUS

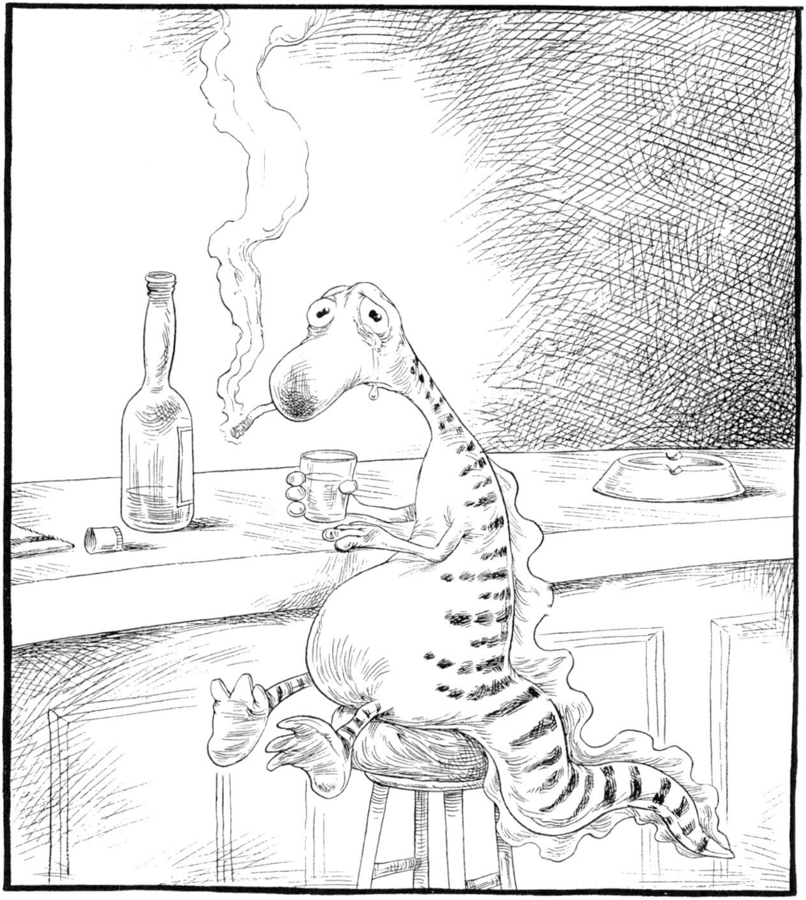

TENDER IS THE NEWT

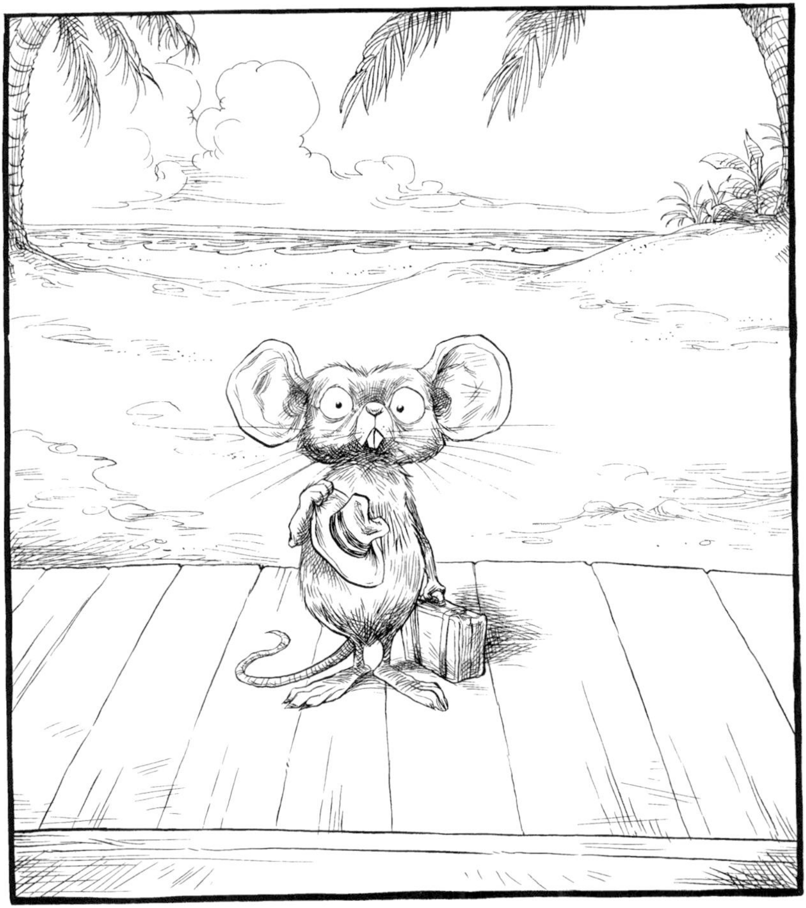

A Mouse for Mr. Biswas

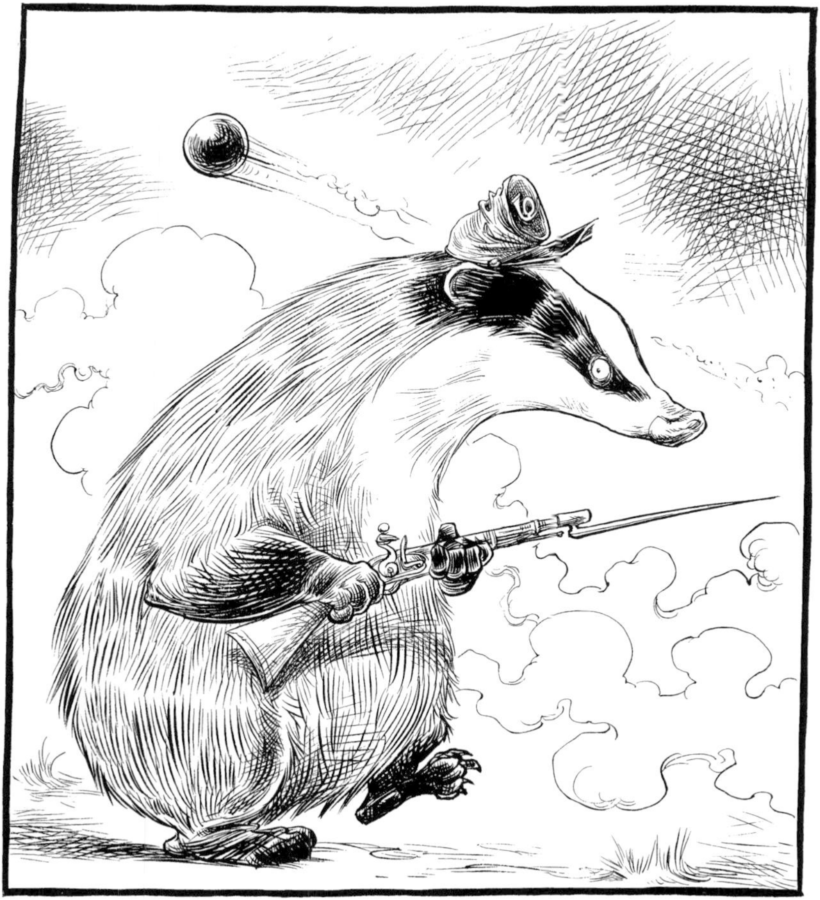

THE RED BADGER OF COURAGE

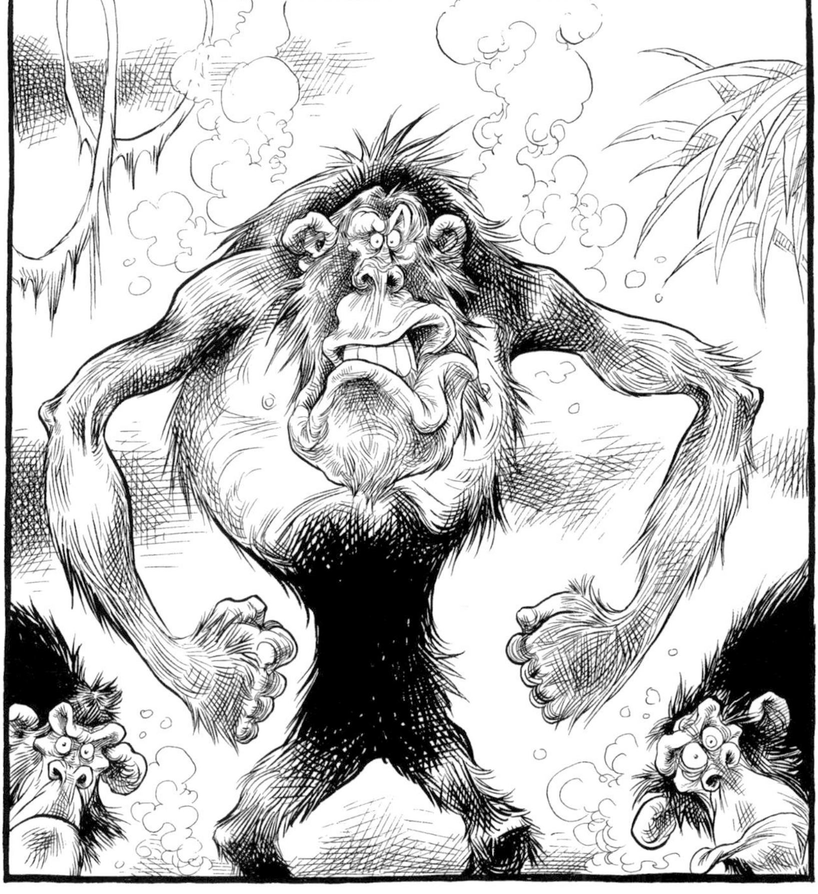

THE APES OF WRATH

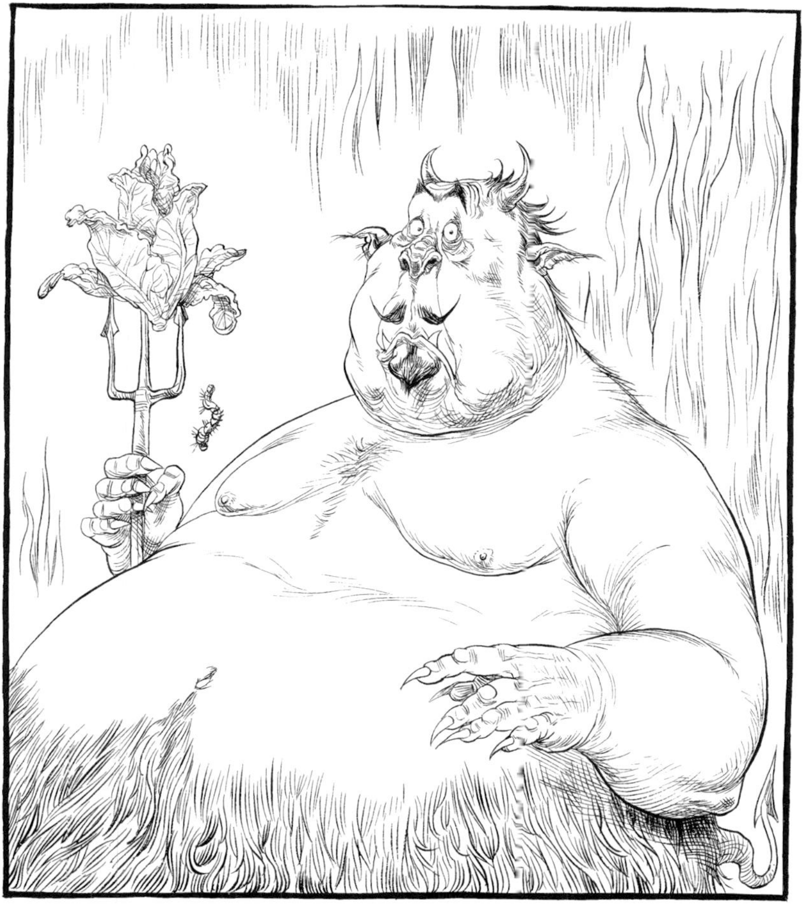

THE SCREWTAPE LETTUCE

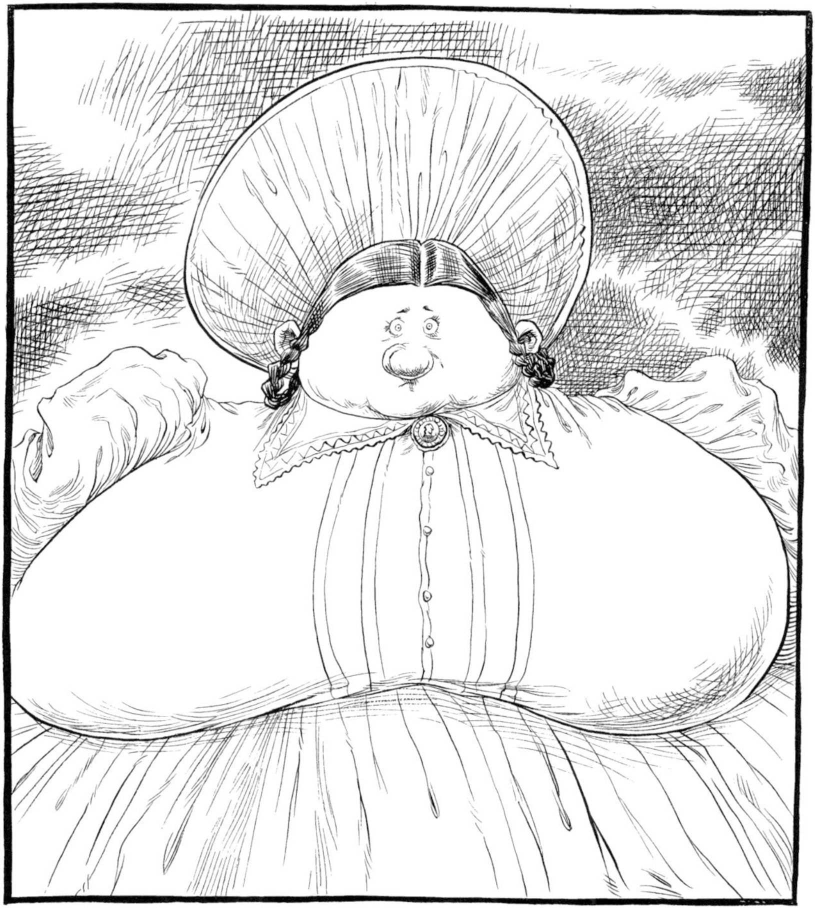

LARGE DORRIT

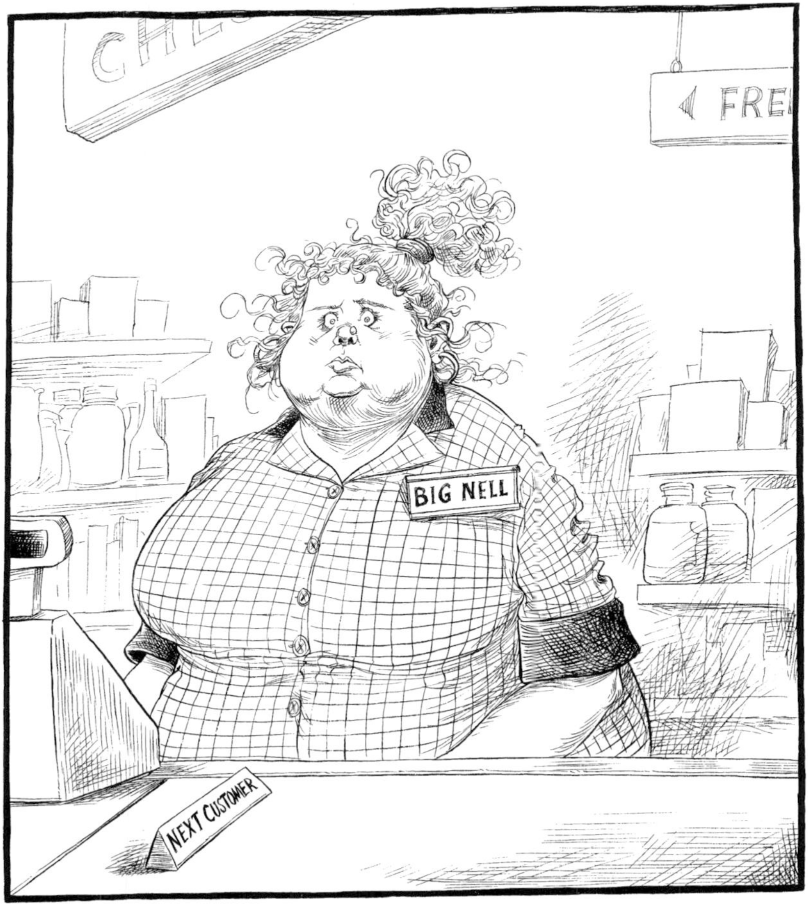
CH
◄ FRE
BIG NELL
NEXT CUSTOMER

THE NEW CURIOSITY SHOP

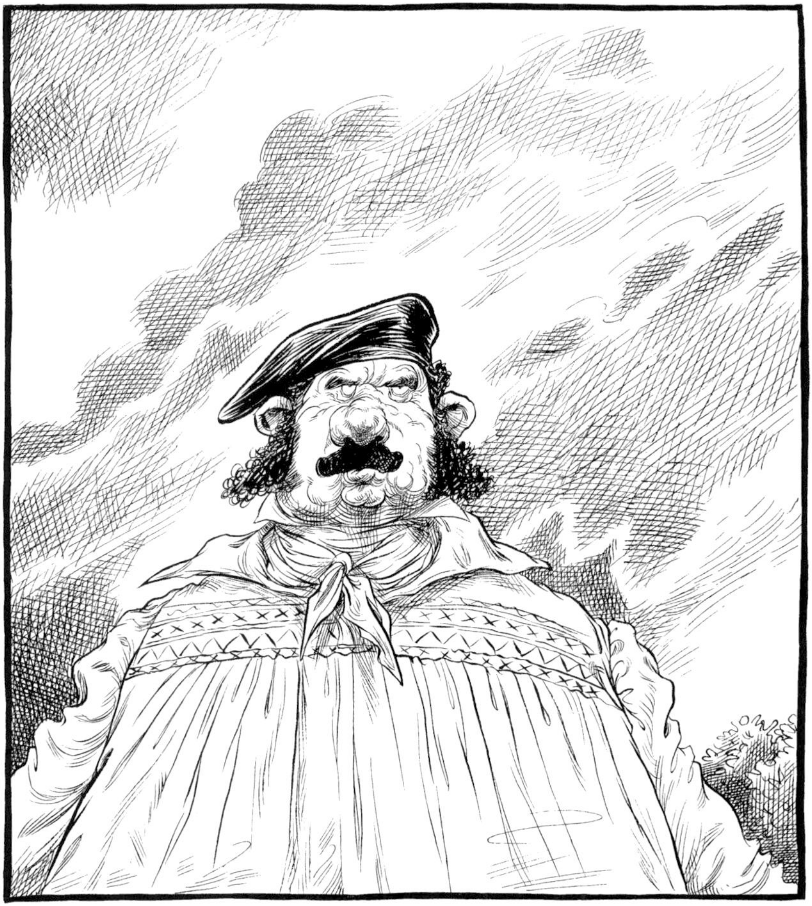

SADDAM BEDE

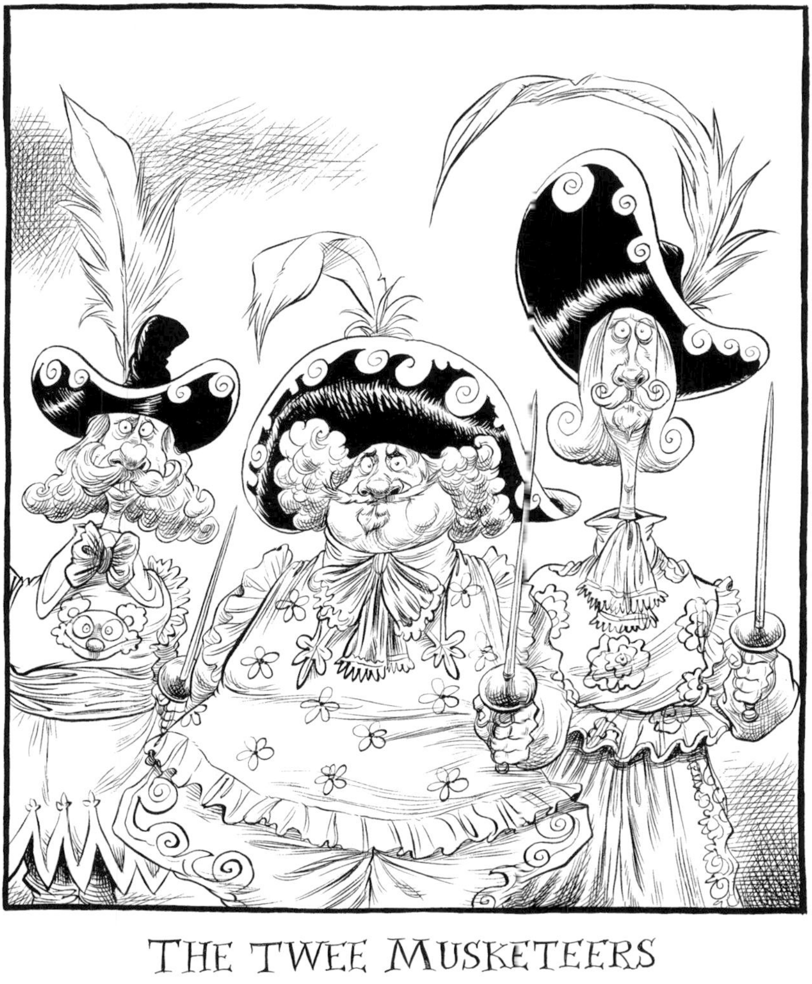

THE TWEE MUSKETEERS

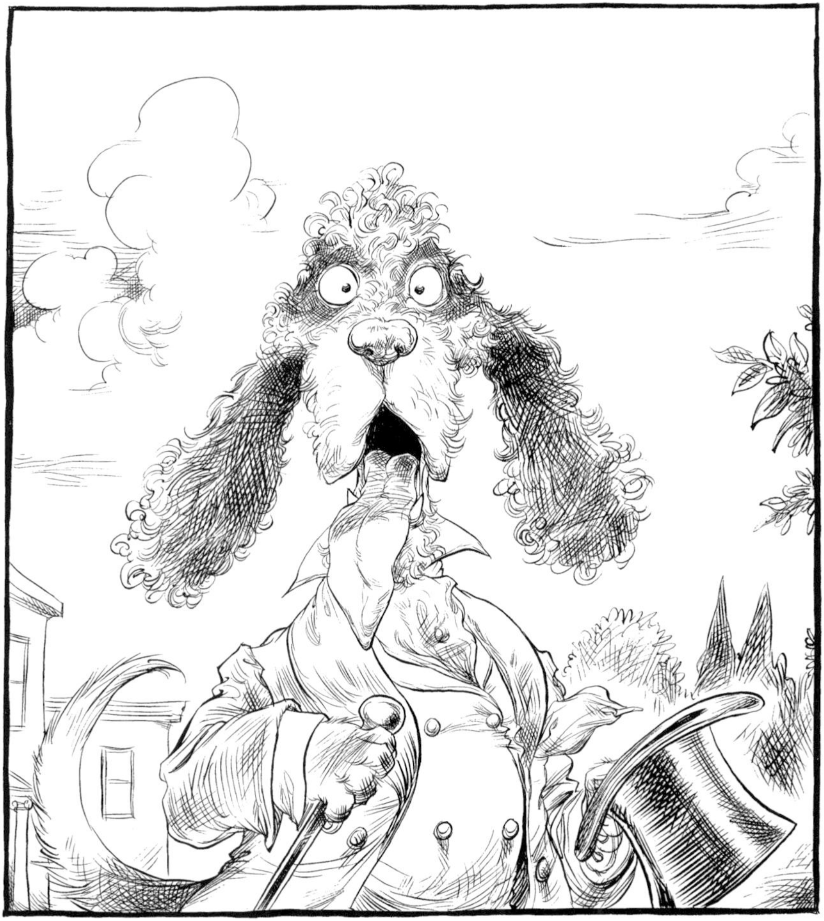

SPANIEL DERONDA

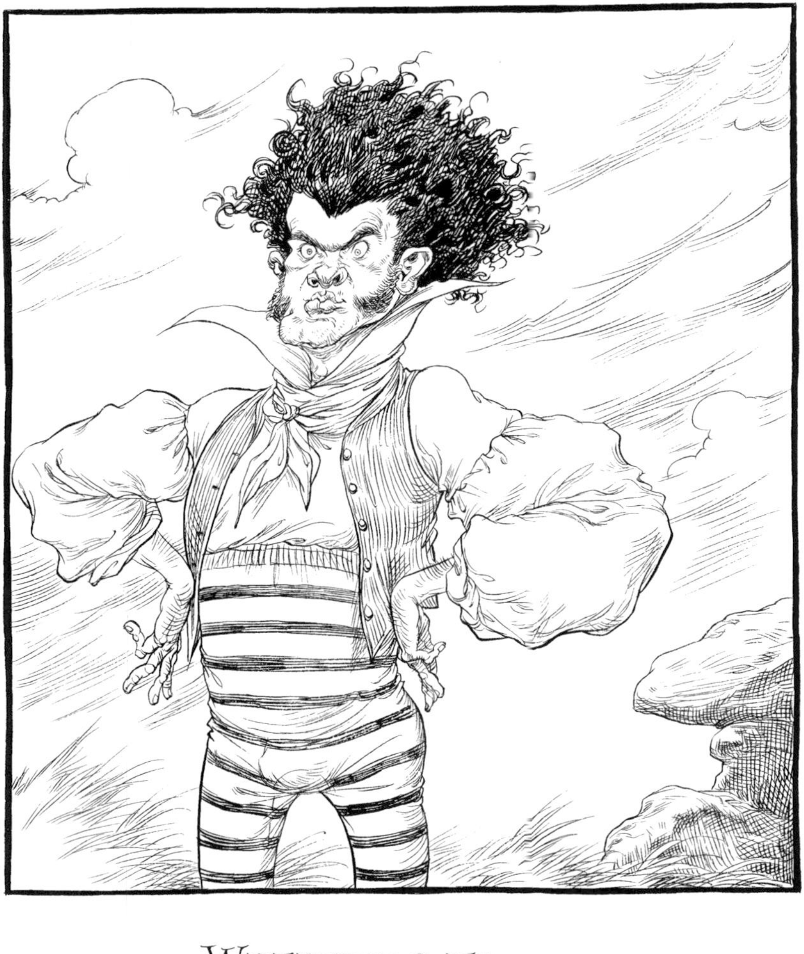

Wuthering Tights

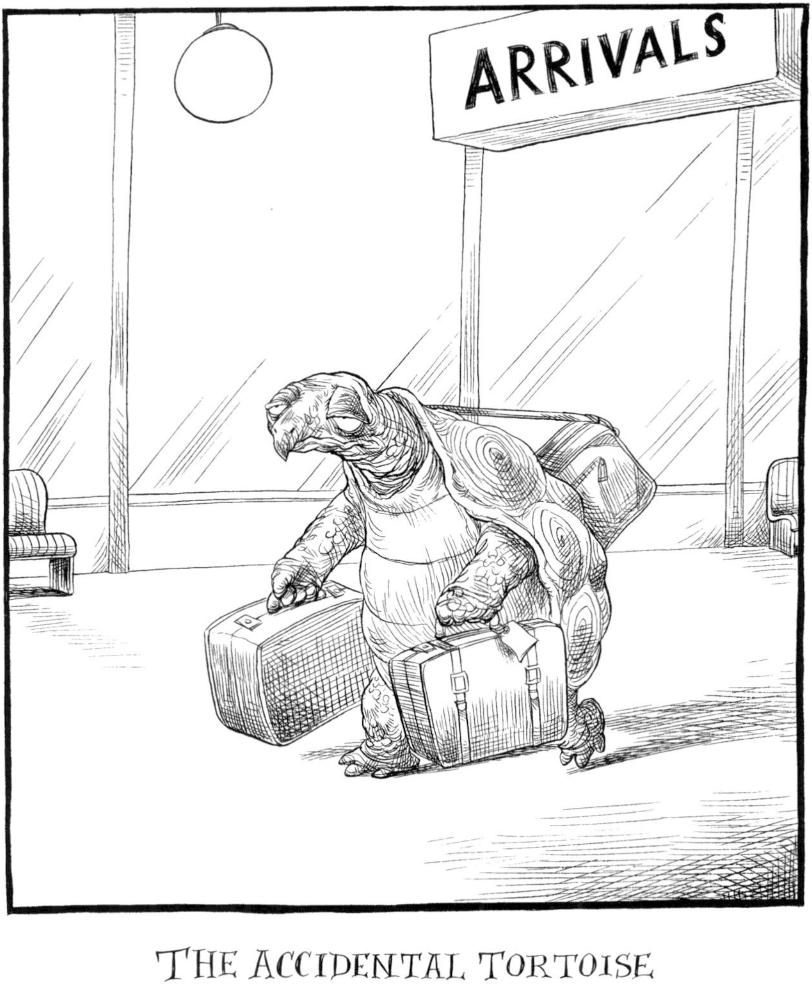
ARRIVALS

THE ACCIDENTAL TORTOISE

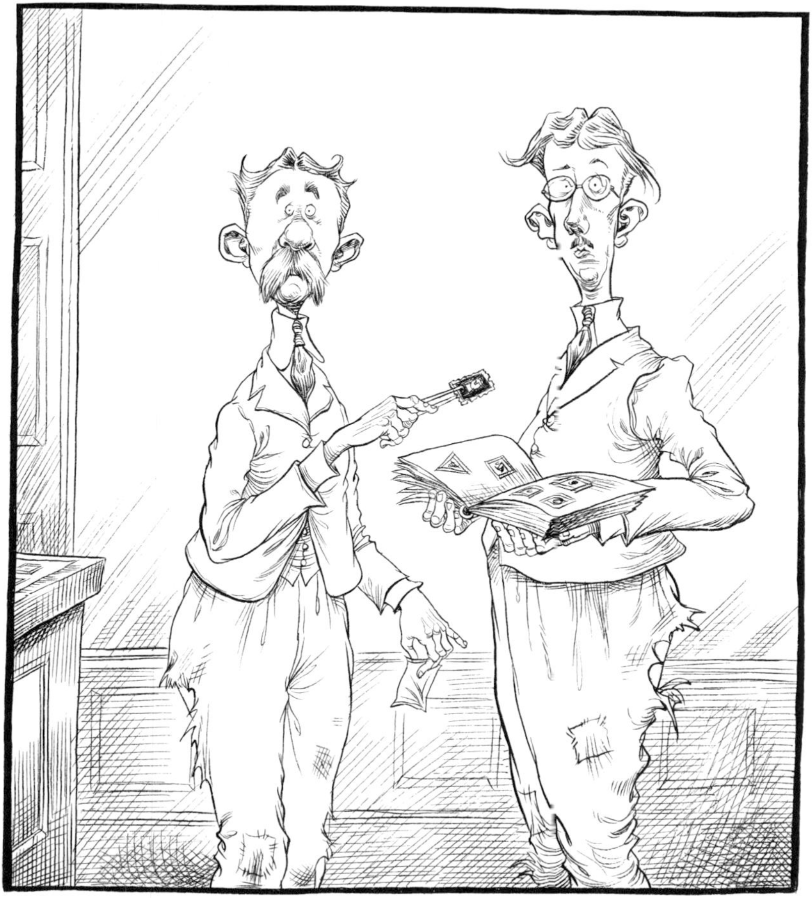

THE RAGGED TROUSERED PHILATELISTS

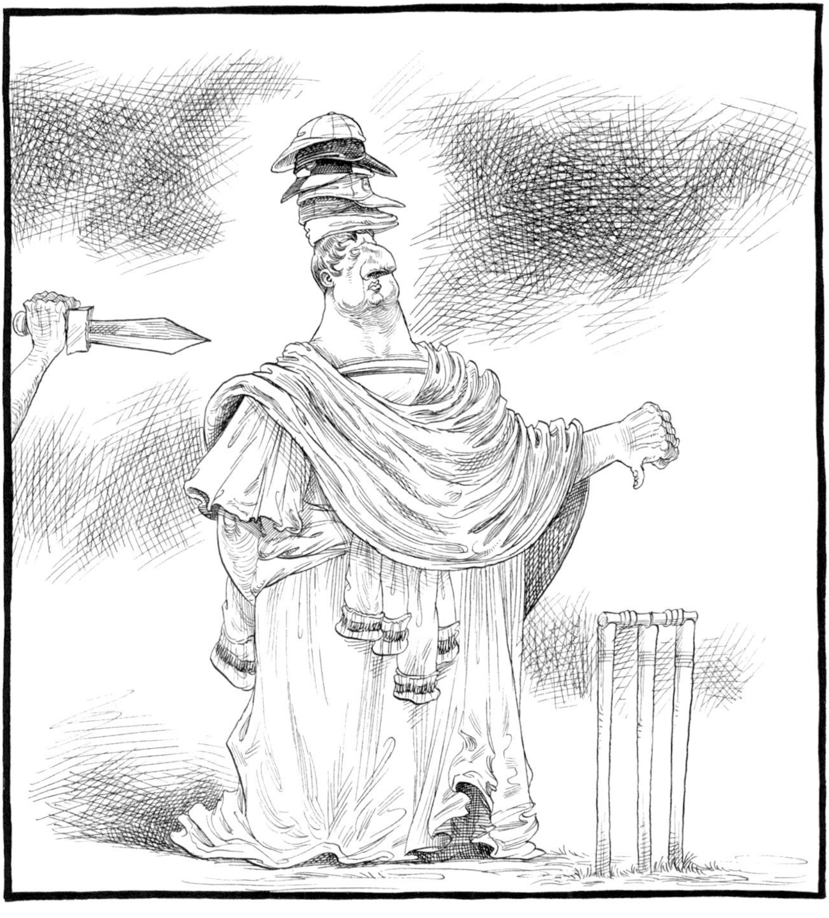

THE DECLINE AND FALL OF THE ROMAN UMPIRE

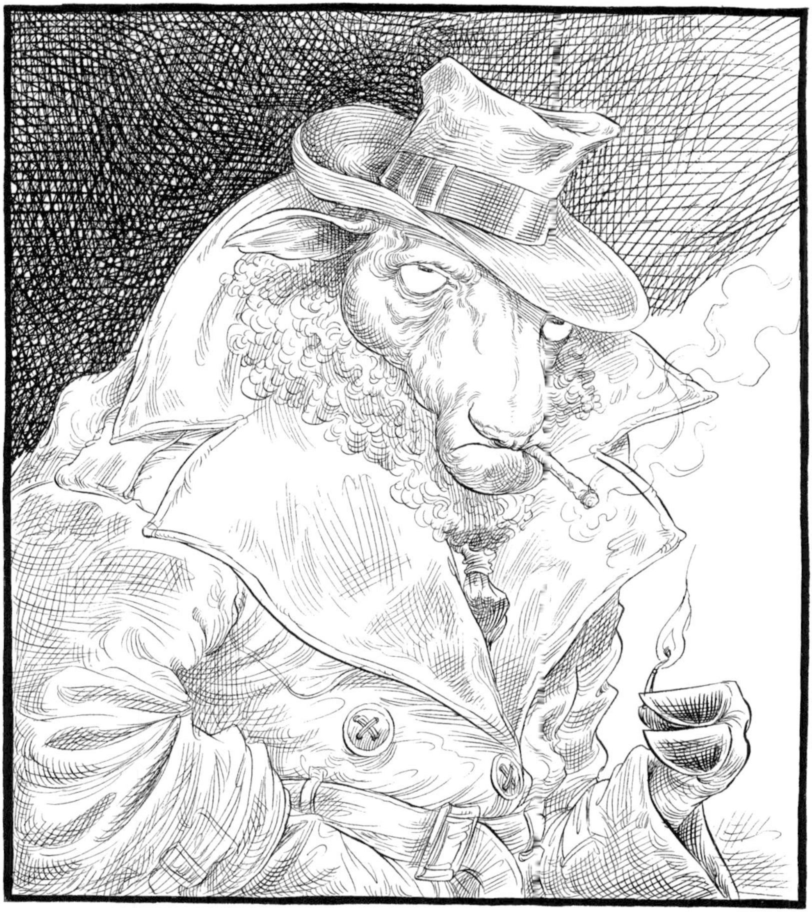

THE BIG SHEEP

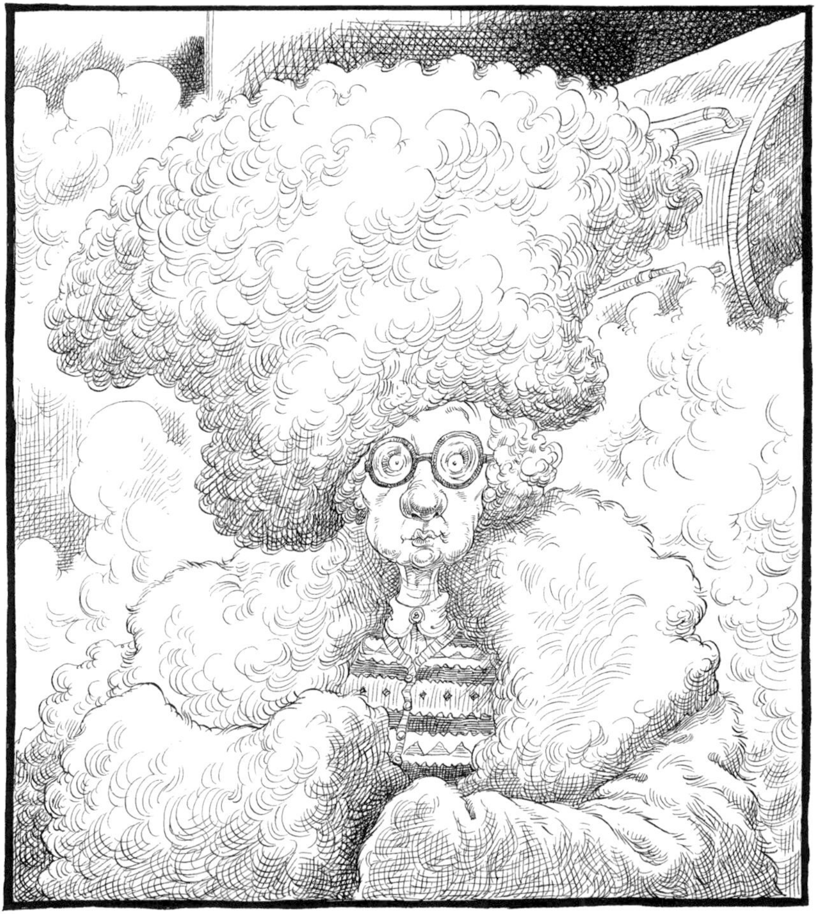

HILDA KARENINA

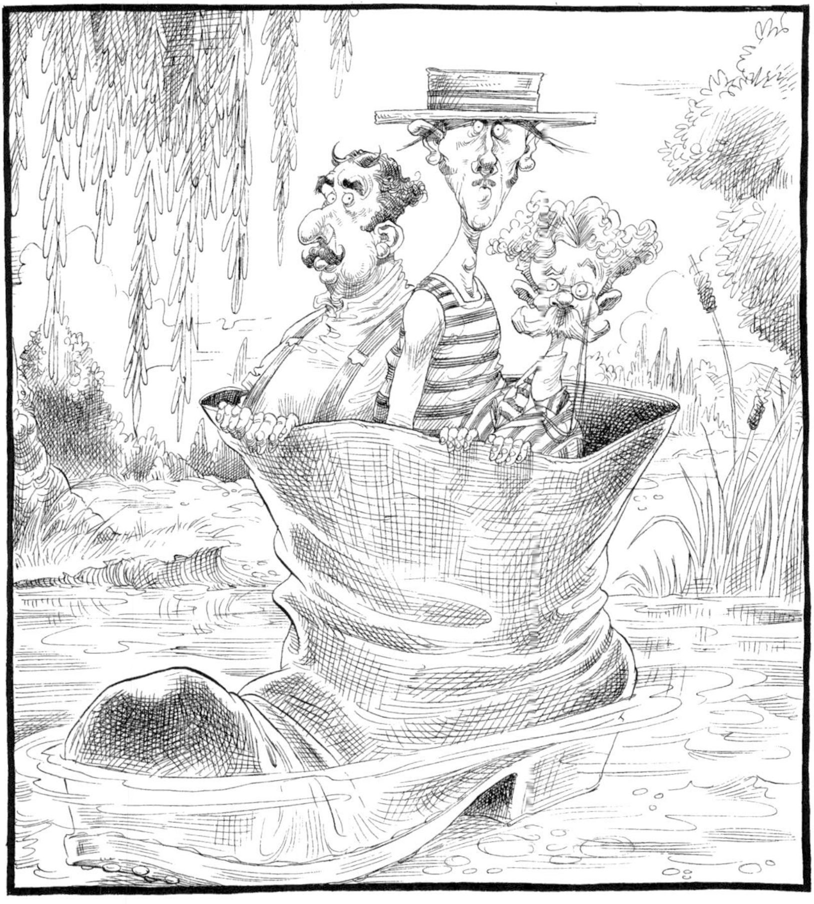

Three Men in a Boot

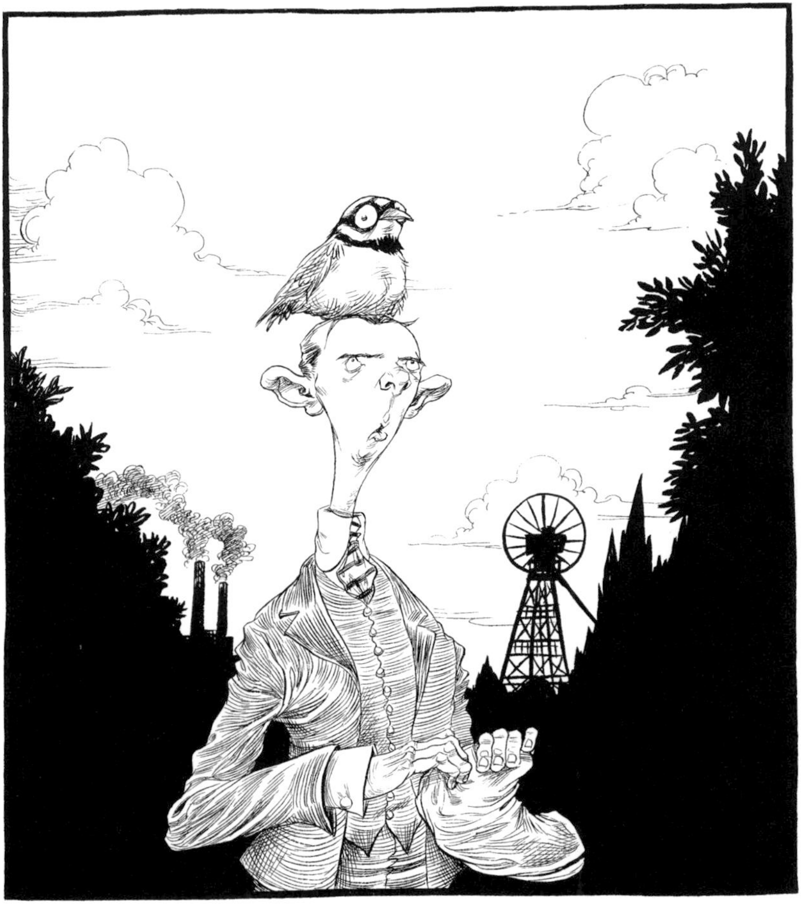

Sons and Plovers

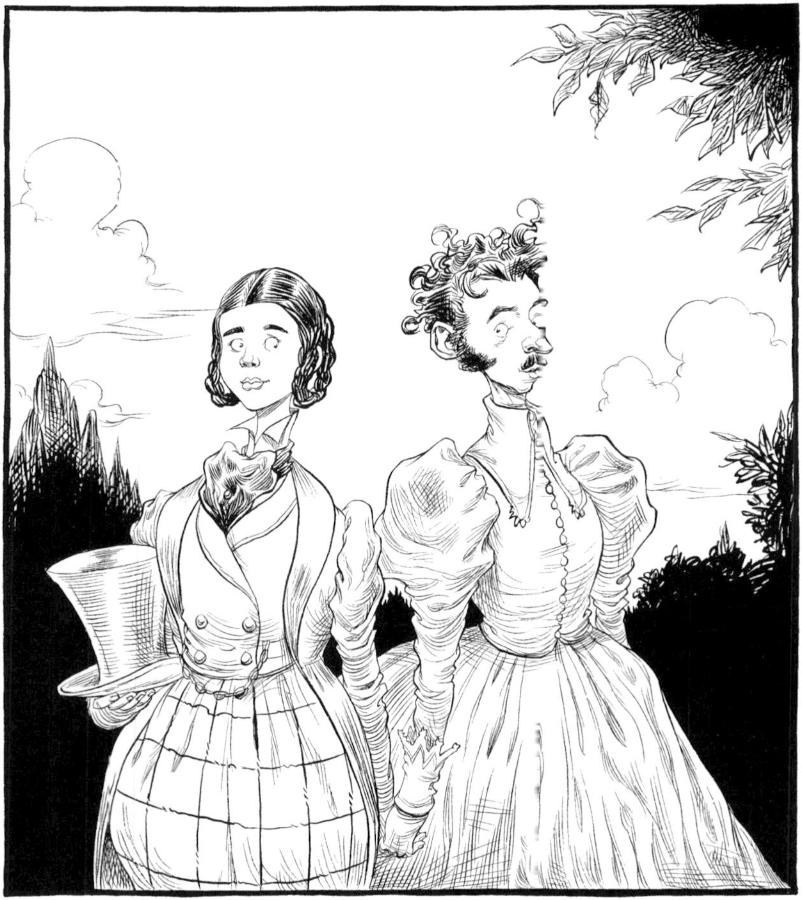

MUDDLEMARCH

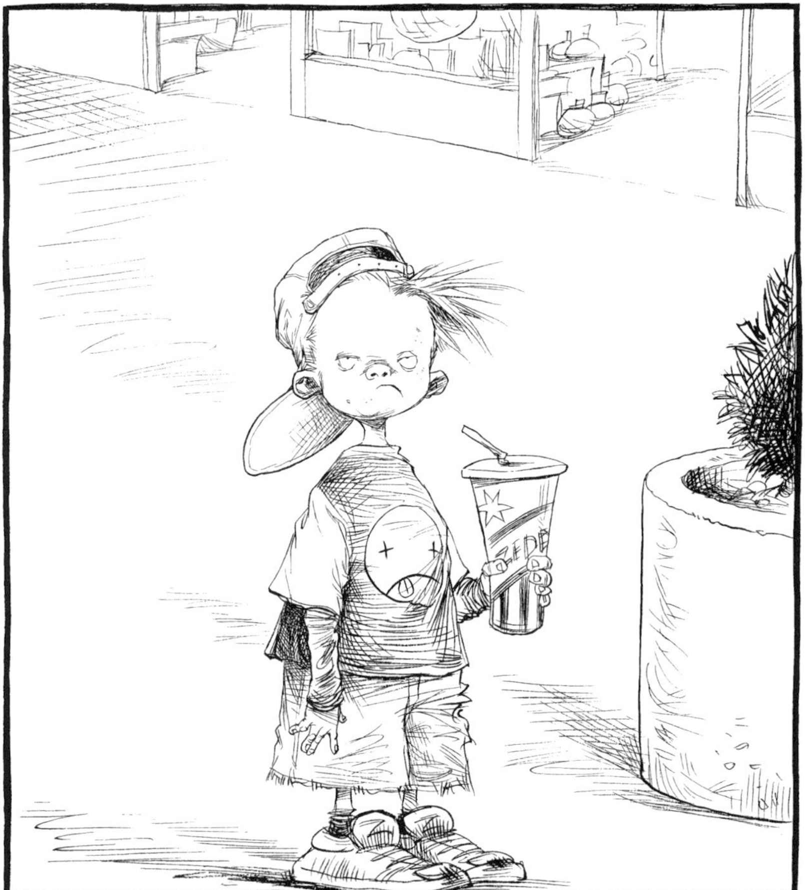

THE TENANT OF WILDFELL MALL

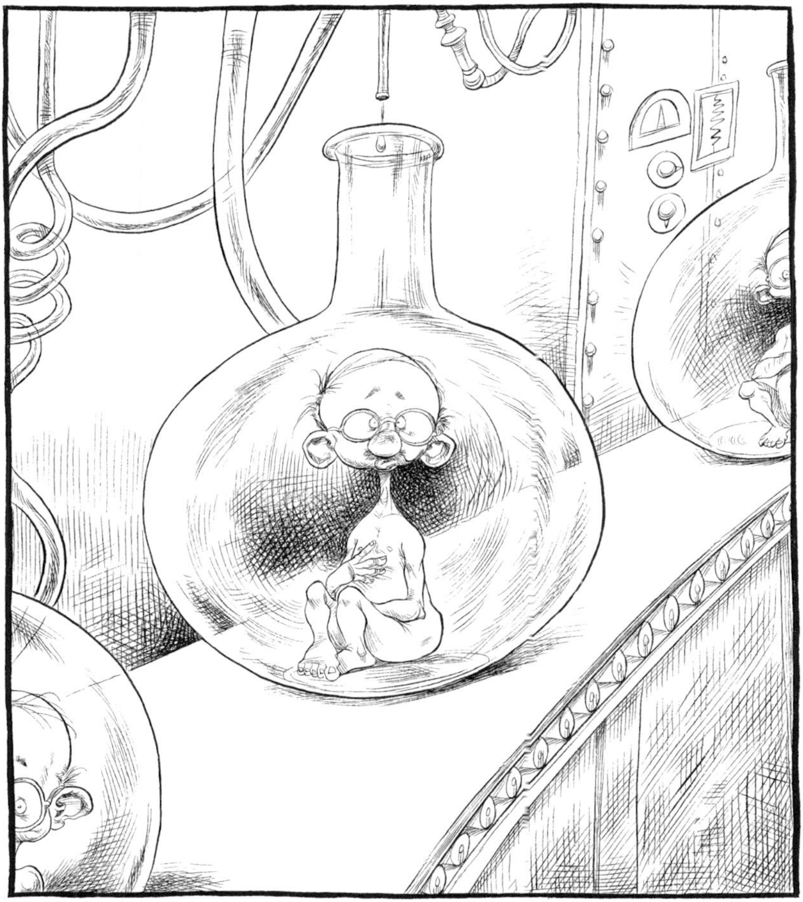

BRAVE OLD WORLD

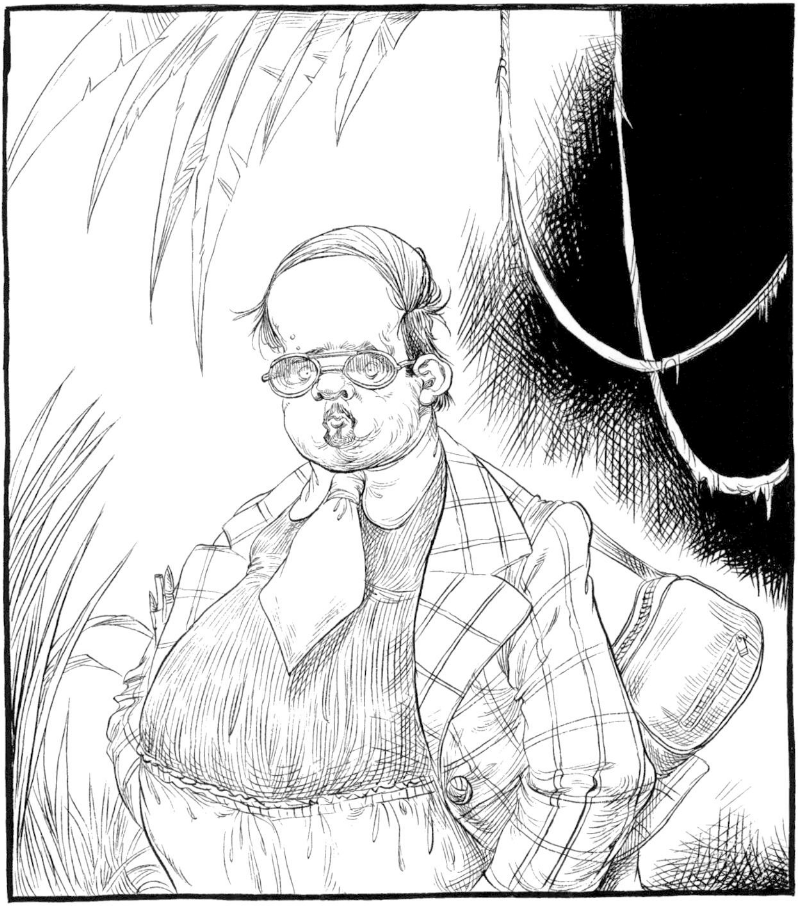

HEART OF DORKNESS

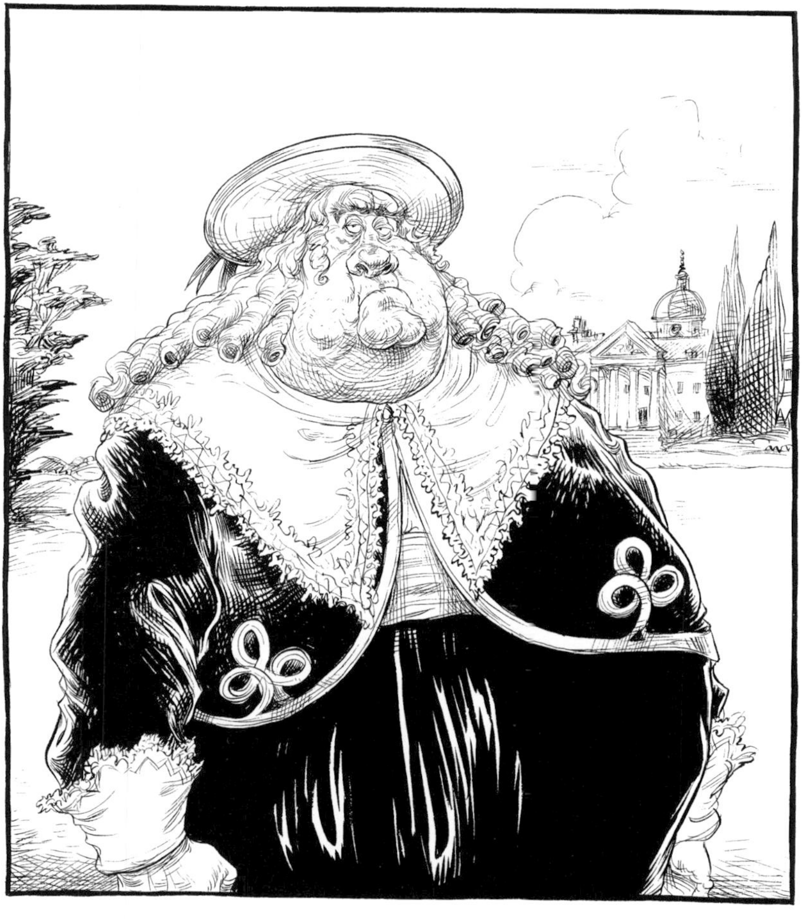

BIG LORD FAUNTLEROY

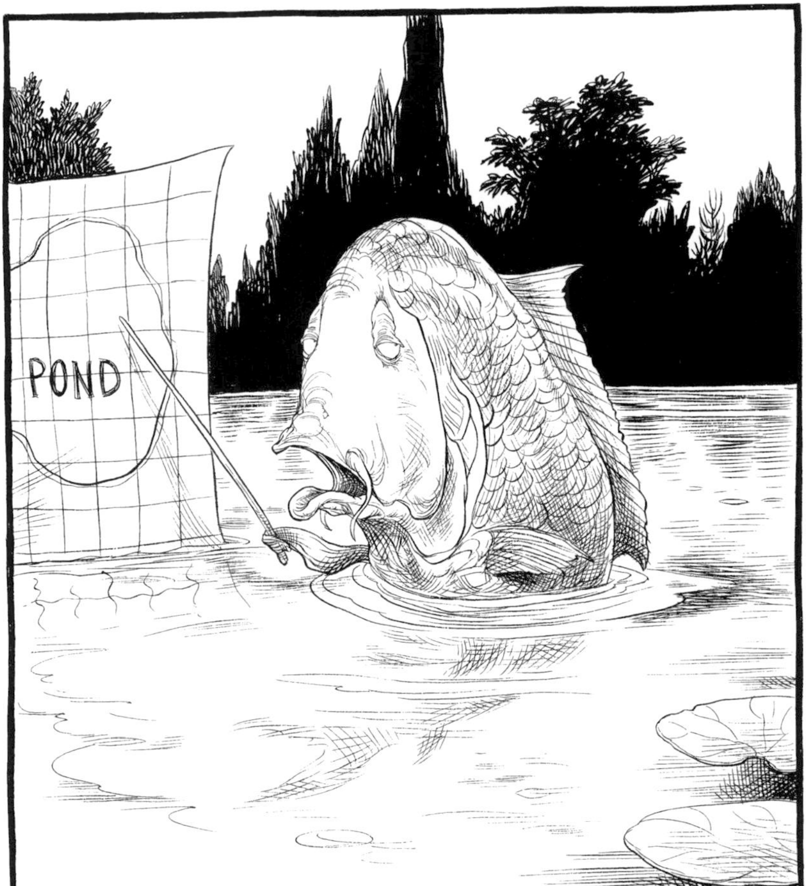
POND

THE WORLD ACCORDING TO CARP

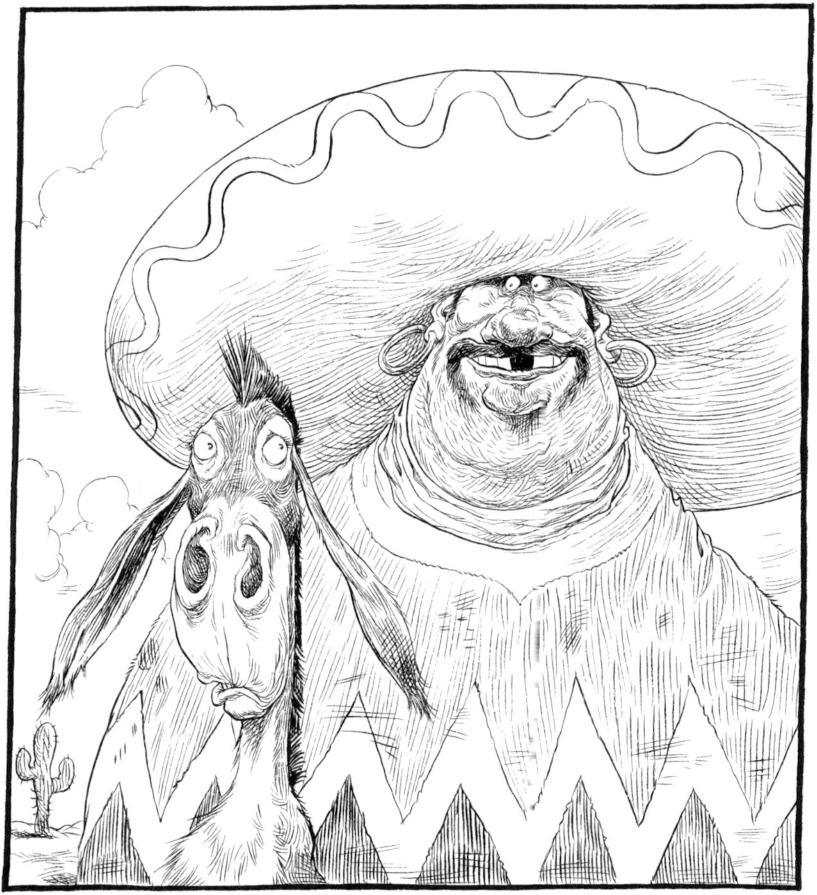

ALL THE PRETTY DONKEYS

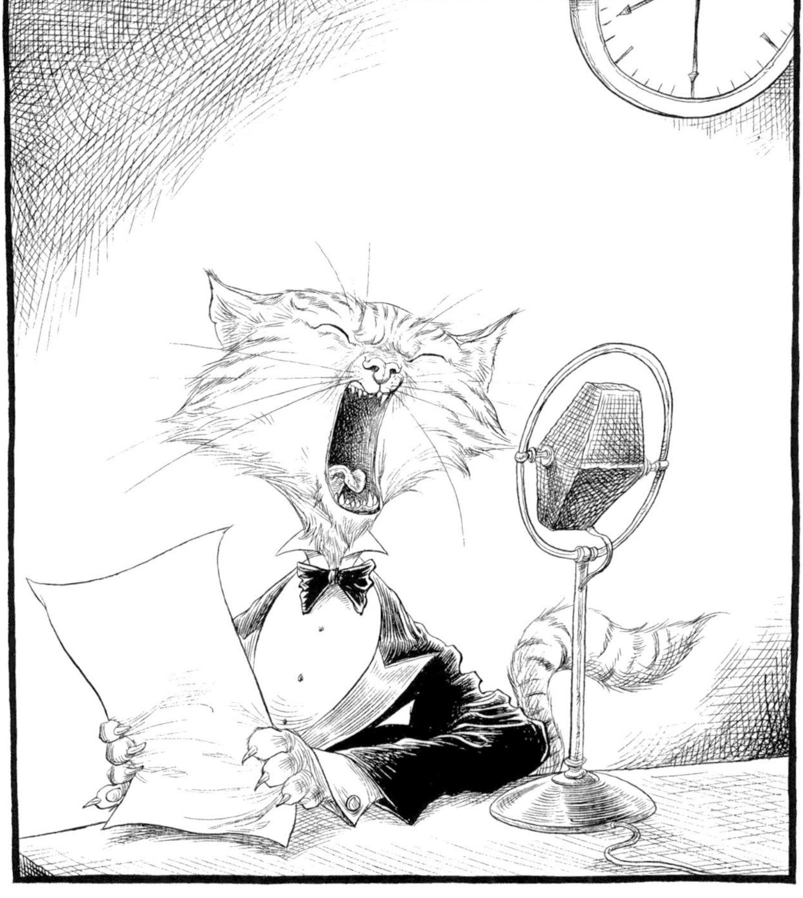

THE SHIPPING MEWS

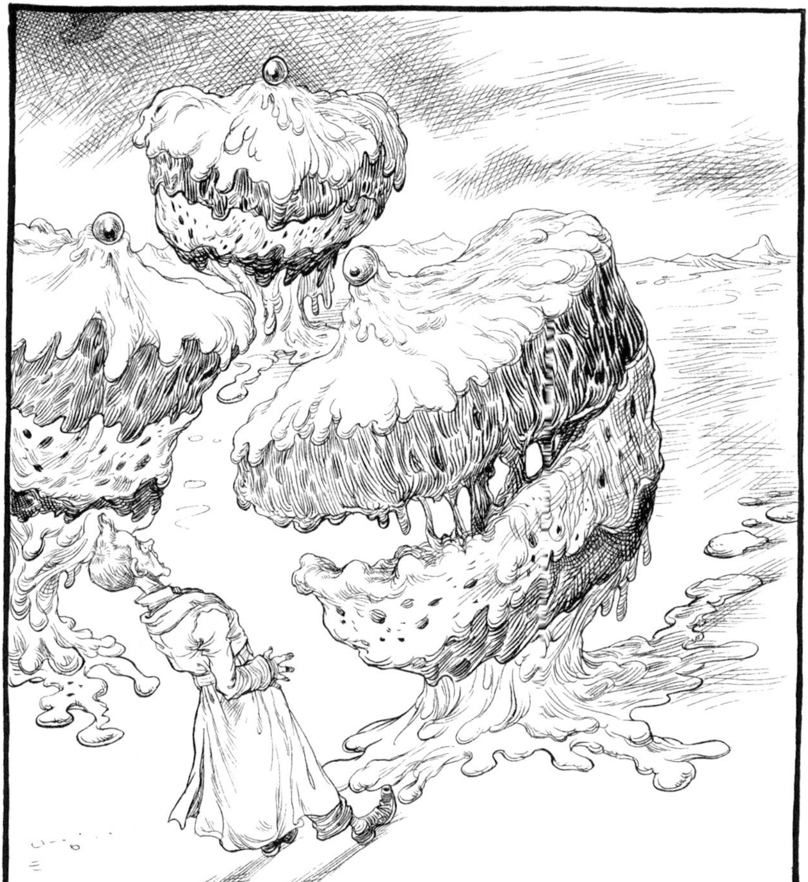

THE DAY OF THE TRIFLES

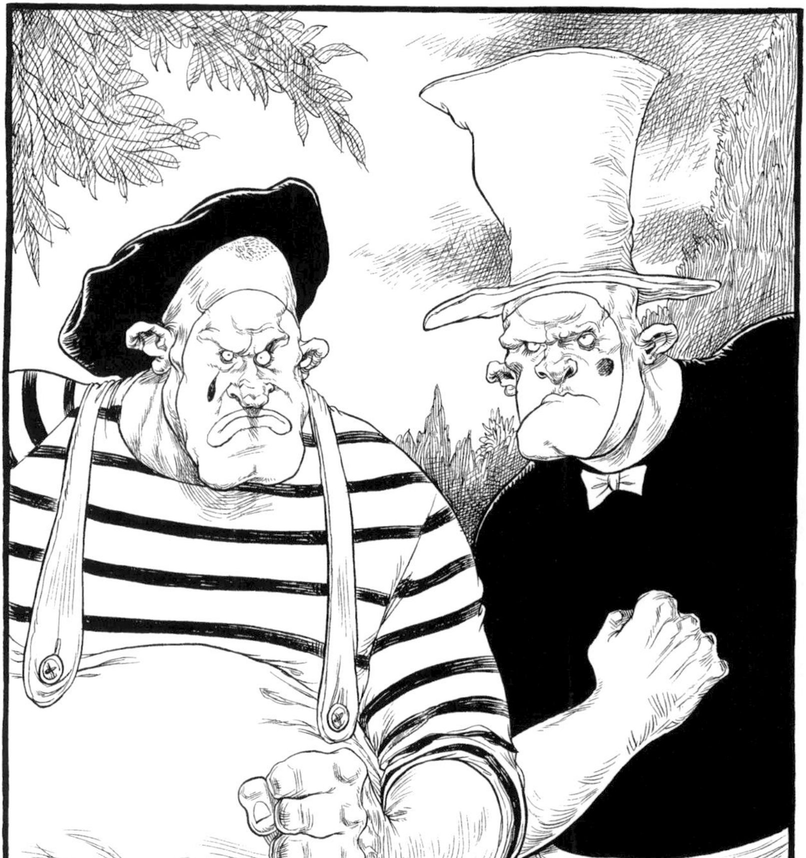

Hard Mimes

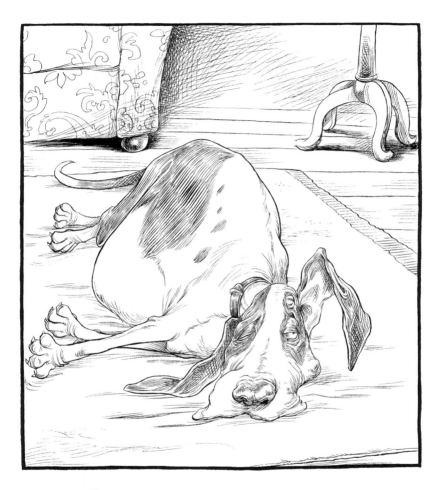

THE NOT-SO-CURIOUS INCIDENT OF THE DOG IN THE DAYTIME

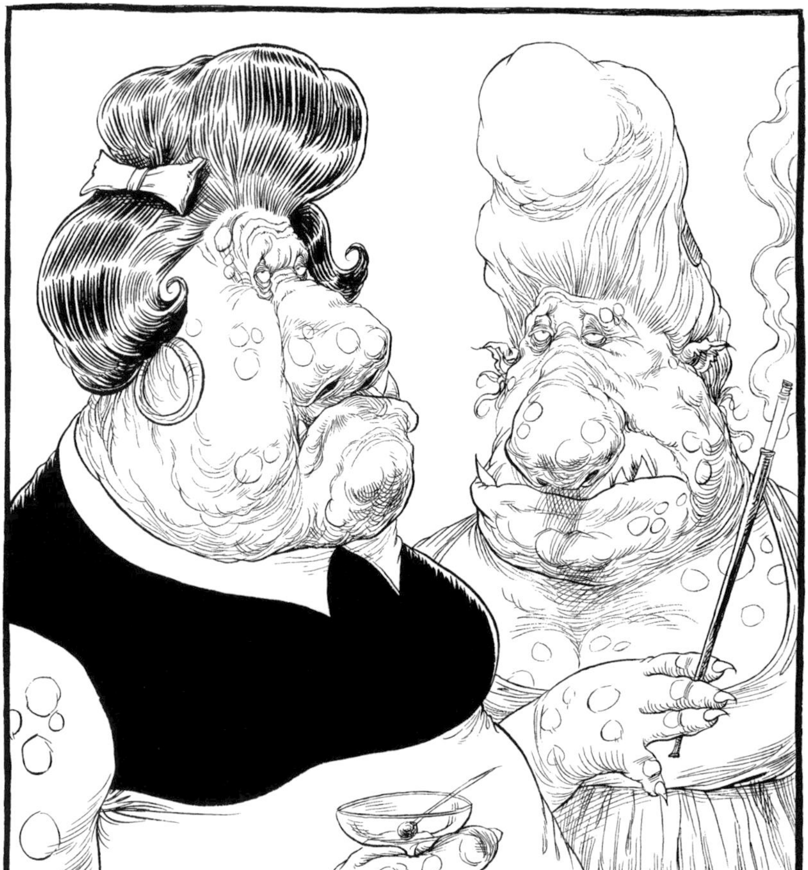

VALLEY OF THE TROLLS

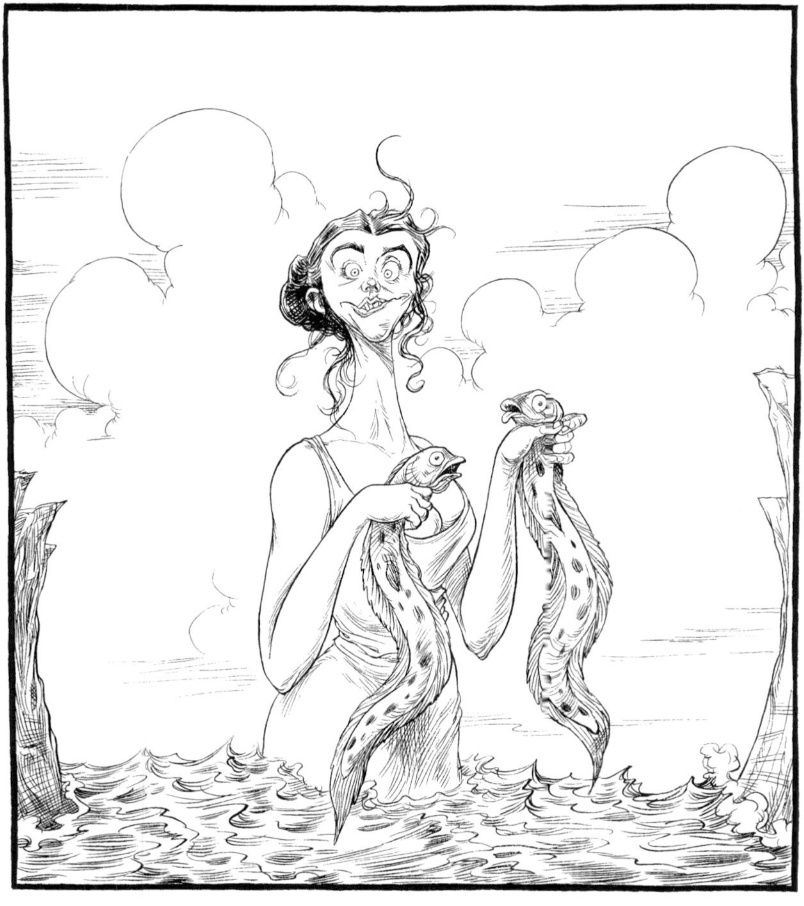

NARROW SARGASSO SEA

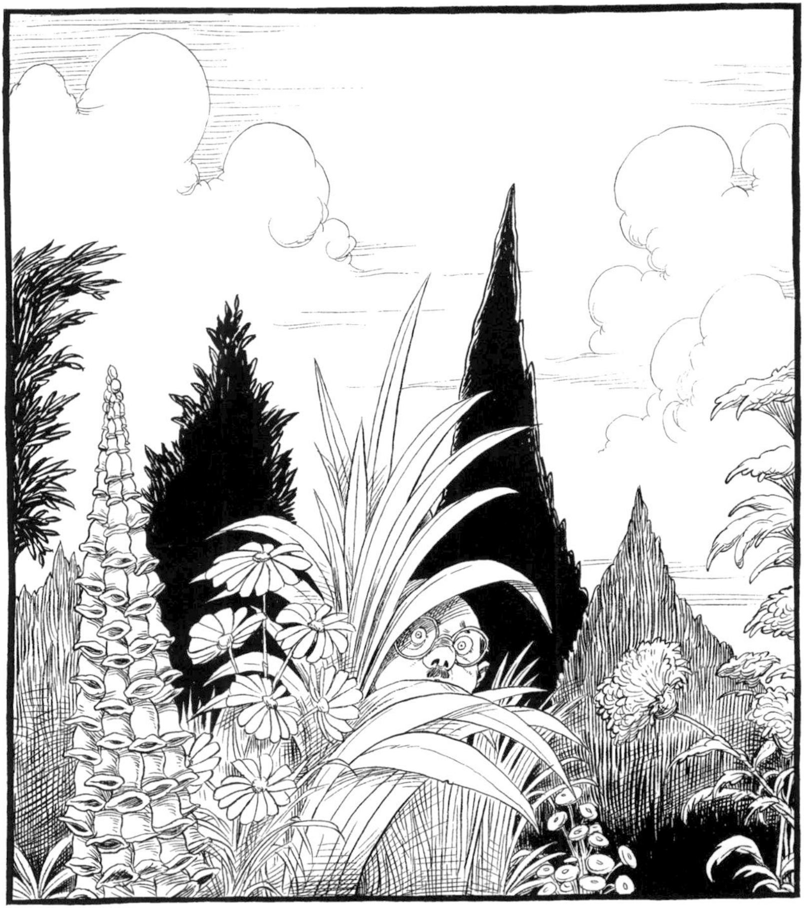

THE SECRET GORDON

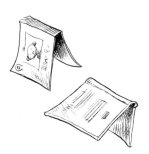

WITH APOLOGIES TO . . .

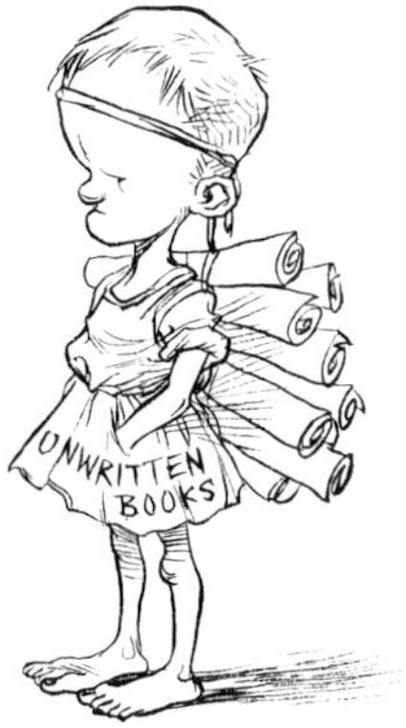
UNWRITTEN
BOOKS

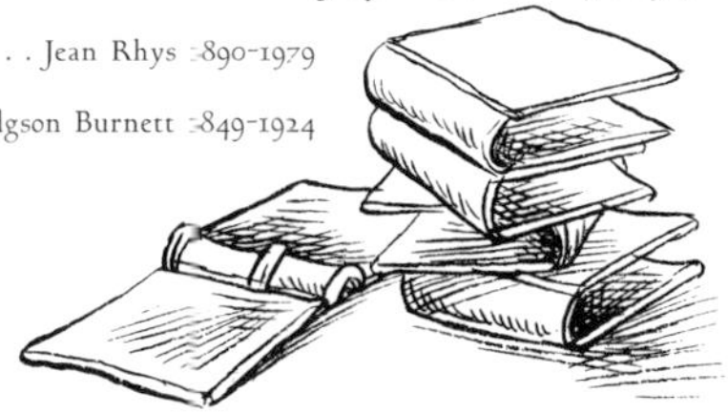

little Miss Greedy

by Roger Hargreaves

Little Miss Greedy certainly was.

What?

Greedy!

I'll say.
As greedy as a giant!
And giants are really very greedy indeed.

Little Miss Greedy lived in Cherrycake Cottage.

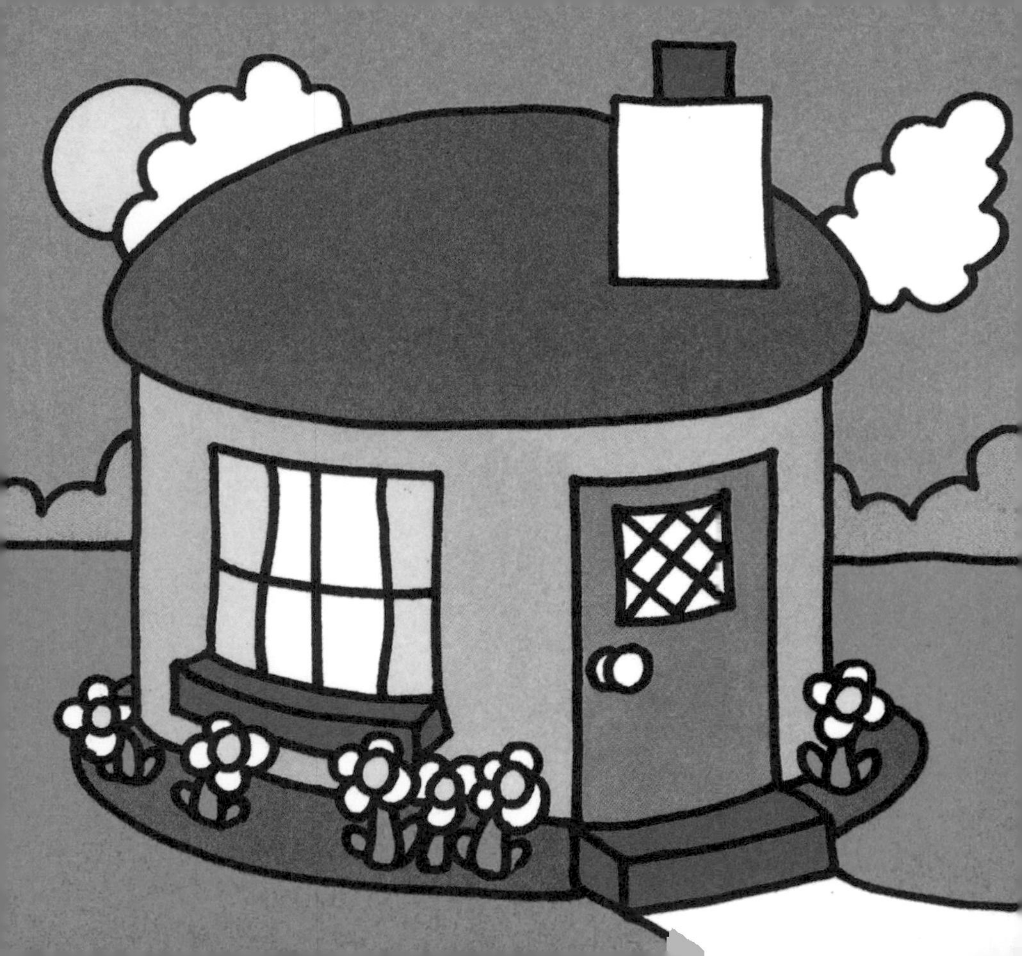

One lovely summer morning, a Monday,
Little Miss Greedy awoke earlier than usual.

She felt rather hungry, and so she went
into her kitchen and cooked herself
some breakfast.

Some breakfast indeed!

Sausages!

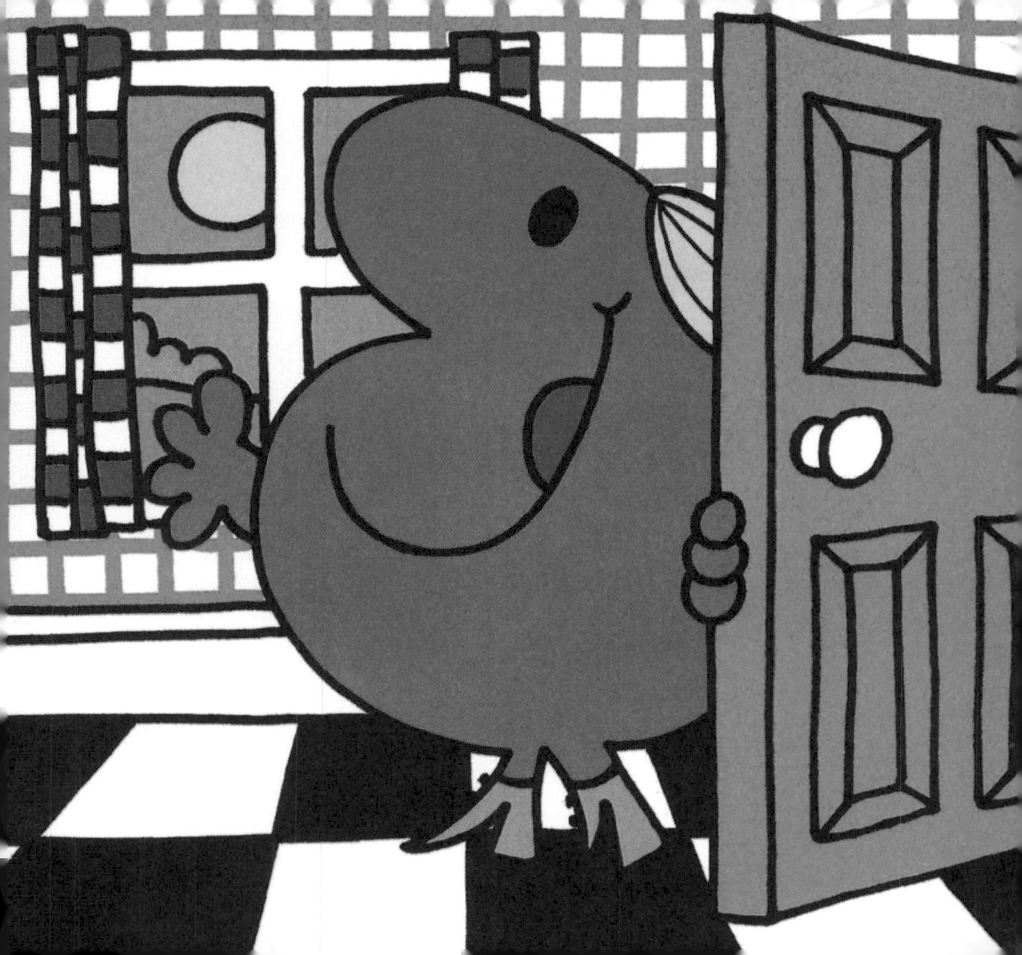

Now if you had sausages for breakfast,
or if I had sausages for breakfast,
how many sausages would we have?

One?
Perhaps two?
Maybe three?

Guess how many sausages Little Miss Greedy
had for breakfast.

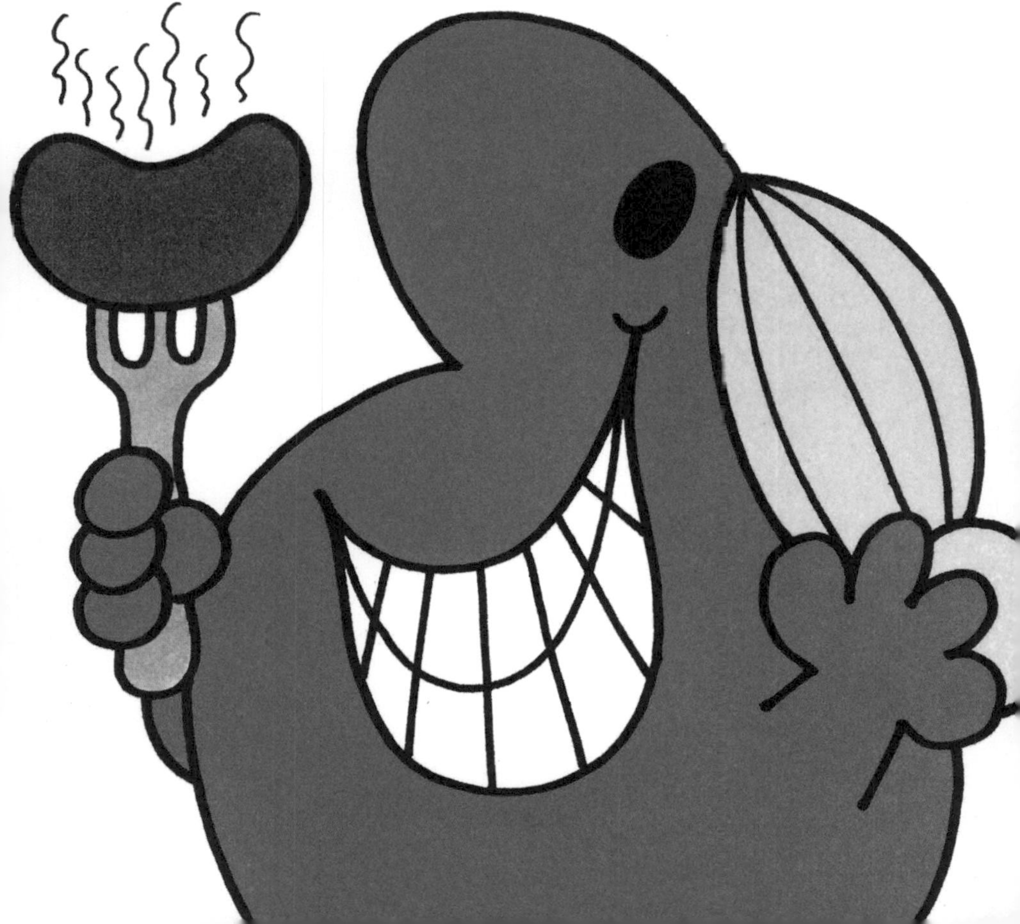

Sixty-six!

Go on, count them!

Sixty-six succulent, sizzling sausages.

Which is difficult to say.

And even more difficult to eat.

Unless you're Little Miss Greedy!

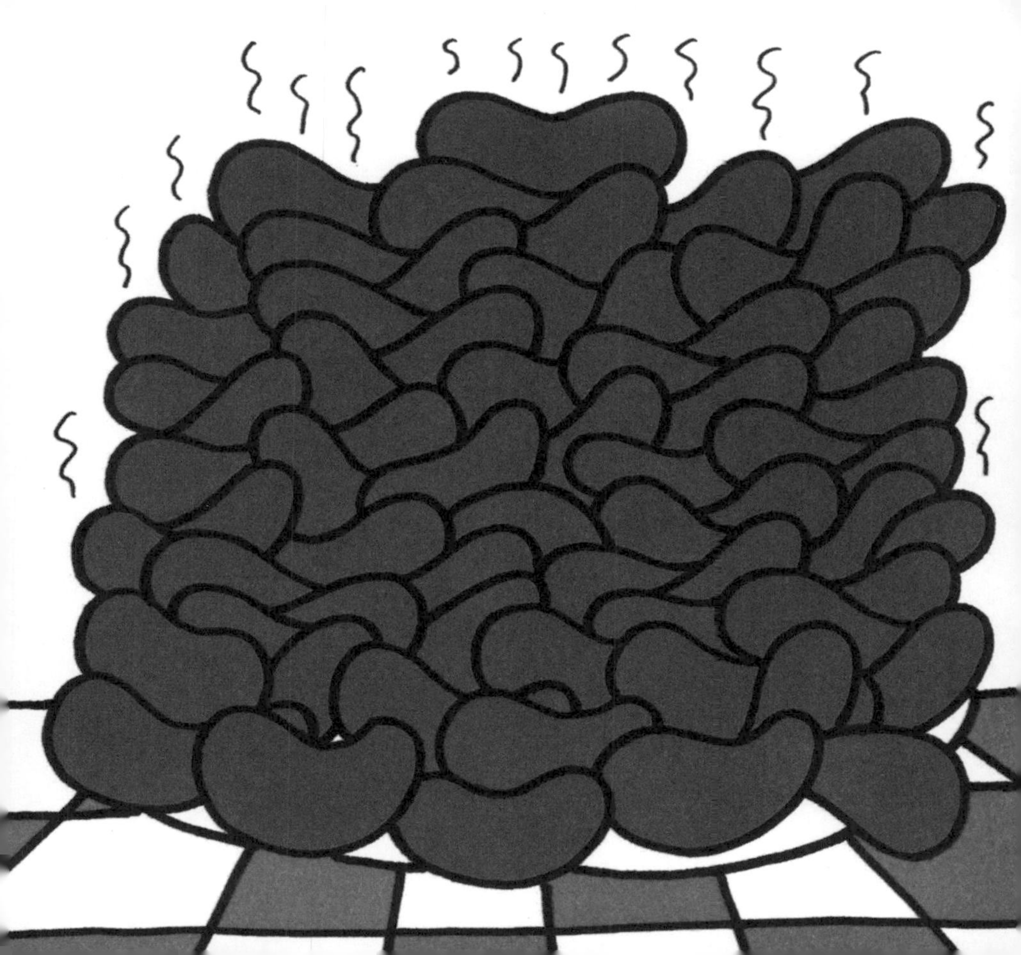

Little Miss Greedy cut the last sausage
on her plate in two, and popped one
half into her mouth.

"Mmm!" she sighed, contentedly.
"That was nice," she thought to herself.
"Now what else shall I have?"

Guess what?

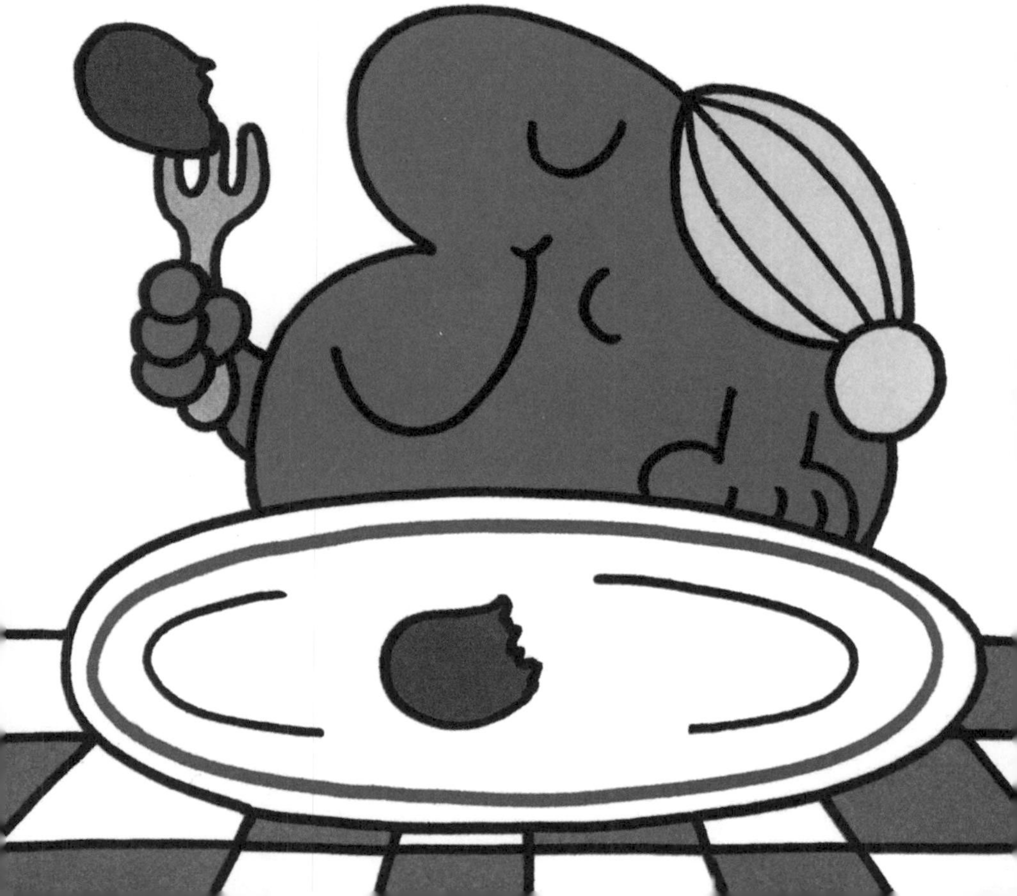

Toast!

Now if you had toast for breakfast,
or if I had toast for breakfast,
how many slices would we have?

Perhaps two?
Maybe three?

Guess how many slices of toast
Little Miss Greedy had for breakfast.

Twenty-three!
Twenty-three thick, tasty slices of tempting toast!
And marmalade.

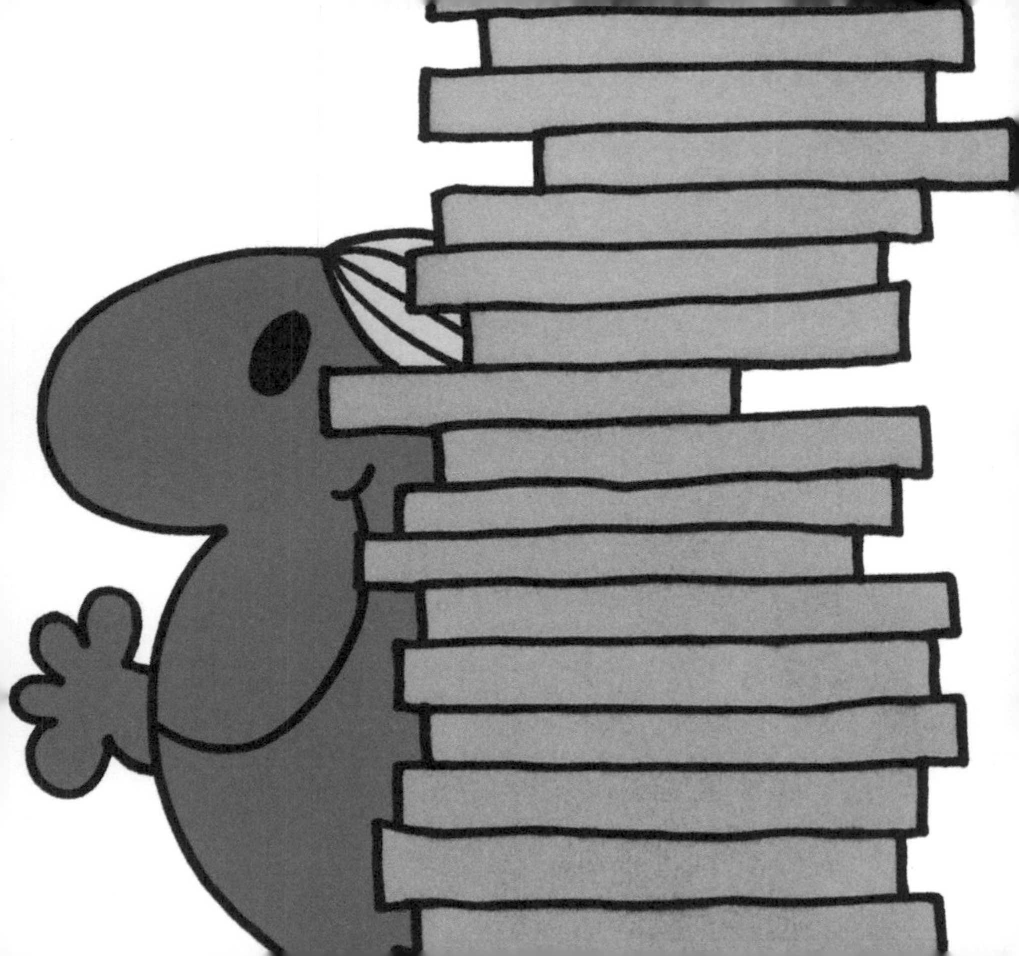

Just as Little Miss Greedy was licking
the last crumb of the twenty-third slice
of toast from her lips, there was a knock
at the door of Cherrycake Cottage.

It was the postman.

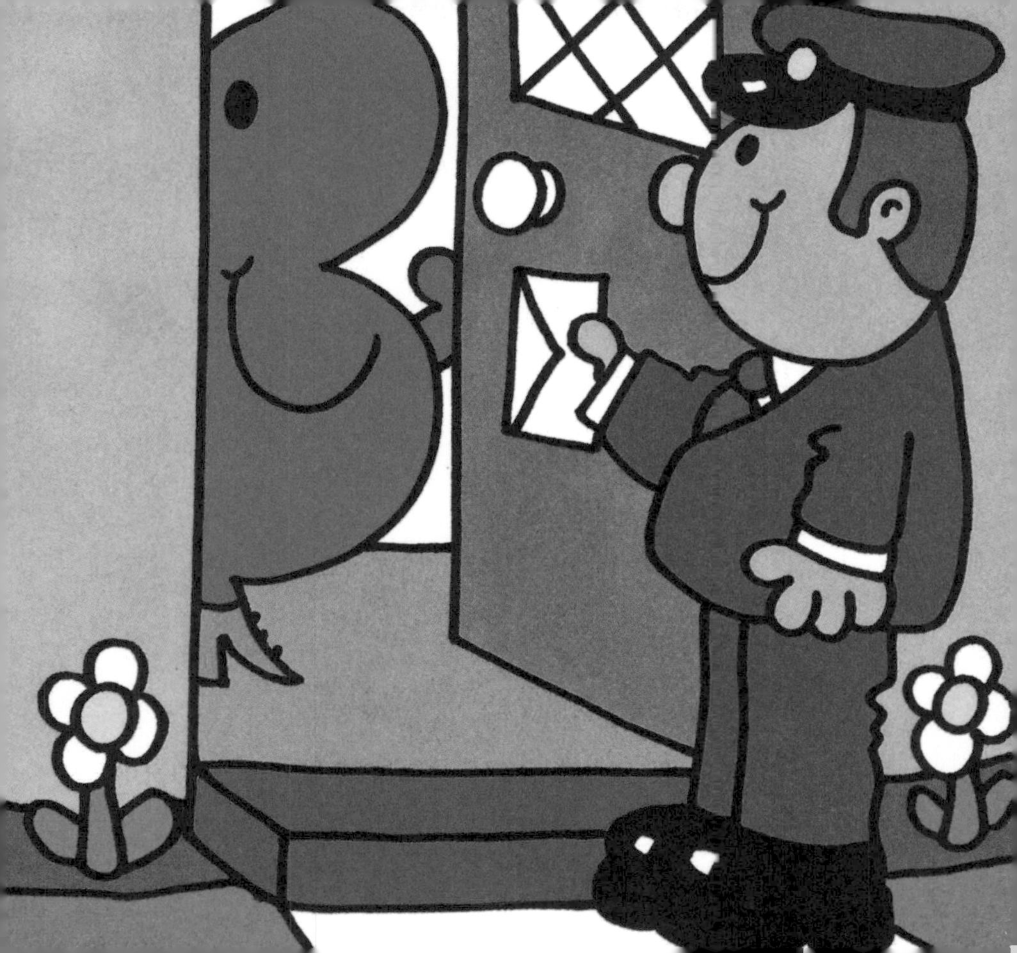

"Letter for you, Little Miss Greedy," he said, cheerfully.

"Oh good," smiled Little Miss Greedy,
for she liked it when someone sent her a letter.

"Would you like a cup of tea while you're here?"
she asked. "I'm going to have one."

One indeed!

Just look at the size of Little Miss Greedy's teapot!

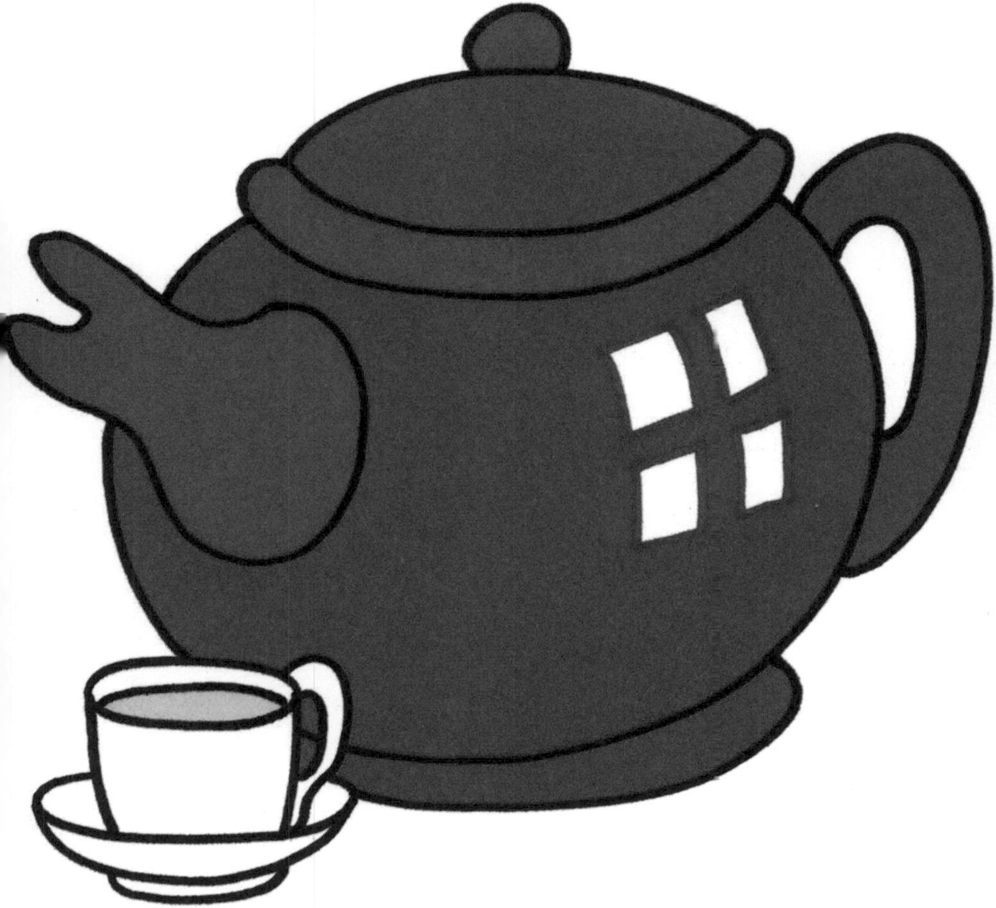

The postman had one cup of tea and a chat, thanked Little Miss Greedy, and left.

Little Miss Greedy poured herself another cup (another after the eleven other cups she'd already had) and opened her letter.

It was from her cousin, Mr Greedy.

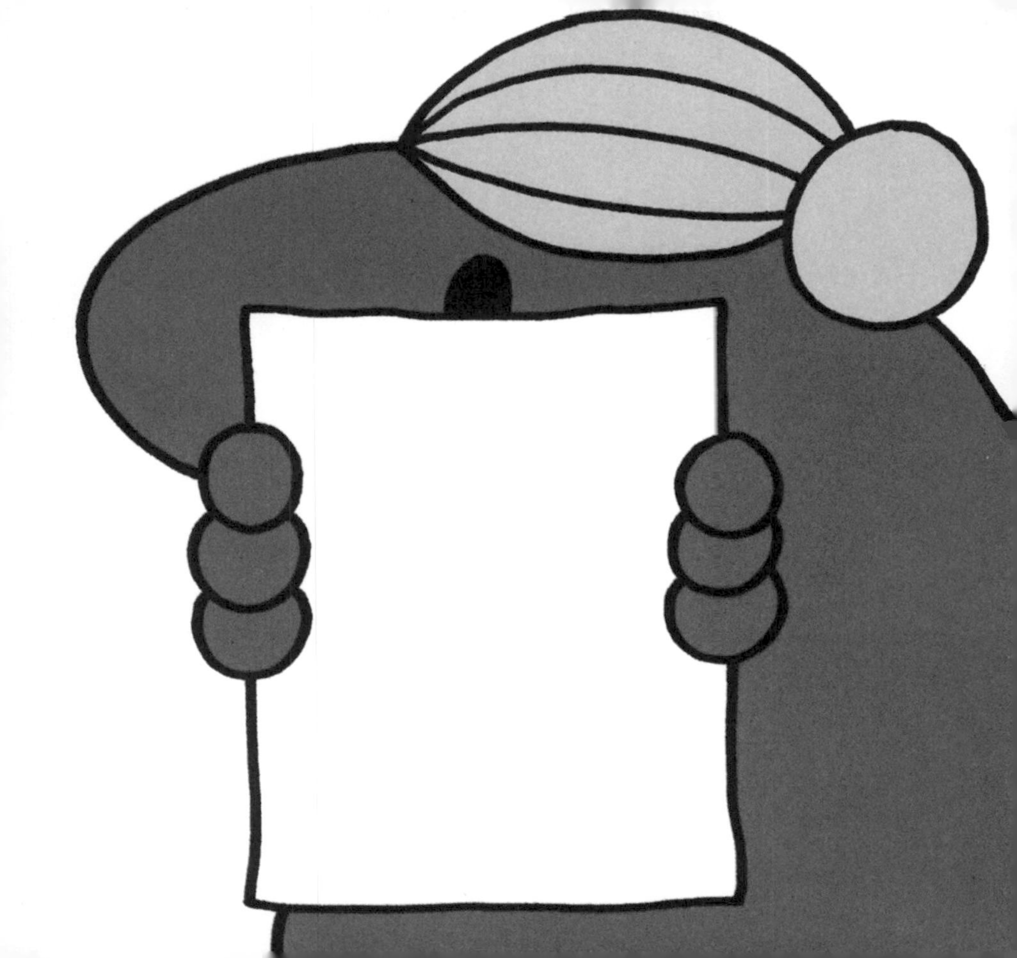

'Dear Little Miss Greedy,' he had written.
(He always wrote to his cousin this way.)

'Next Wednesday is my birthday.
Please come to tea at 4 o'clock.'

Little Miss Greedy was delighted.

She hadn't seen her cousin for
quite some time.

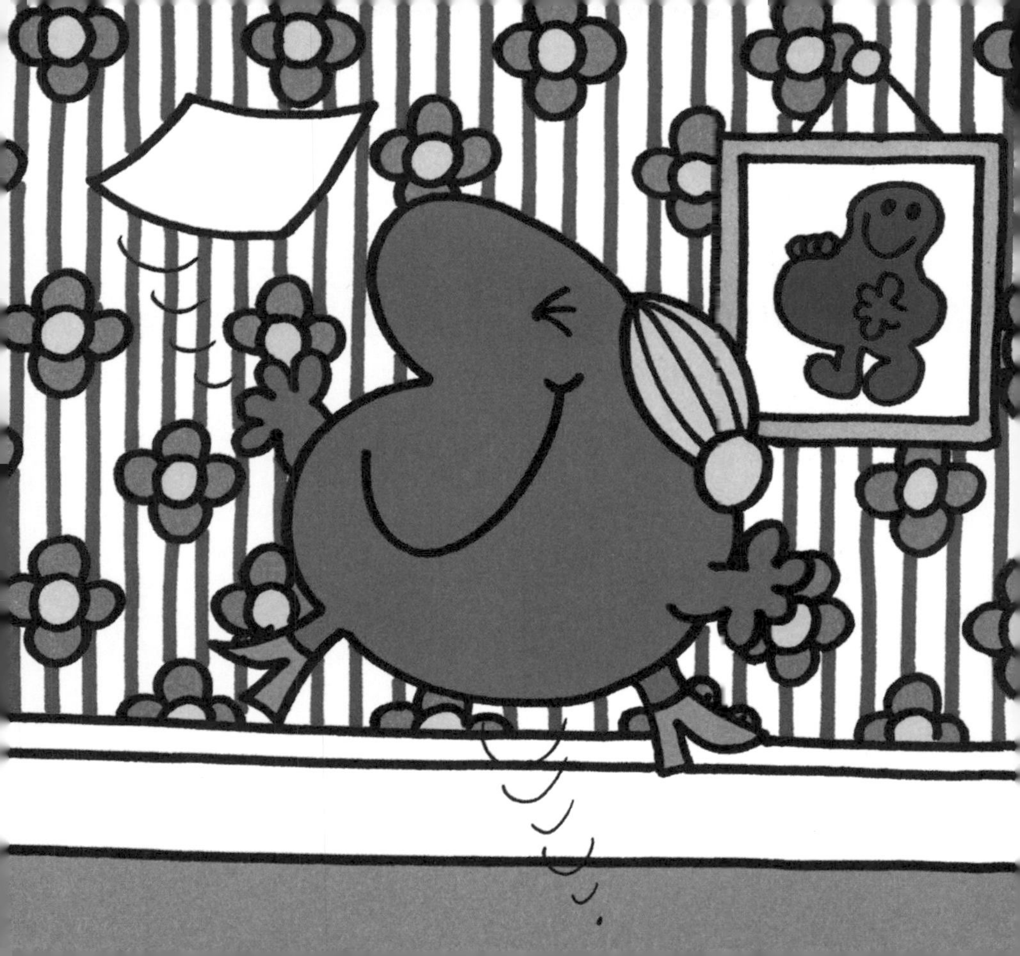

Wednesday was a lovely day.

After a little light lunch (I'll tell you what later),
Little Miss Greedy set off in her car to drive
to Mr Greedy's house.

But before she set off, she put something on
the back seat of her car.

Something large.

Mr Greedy's birthday present.

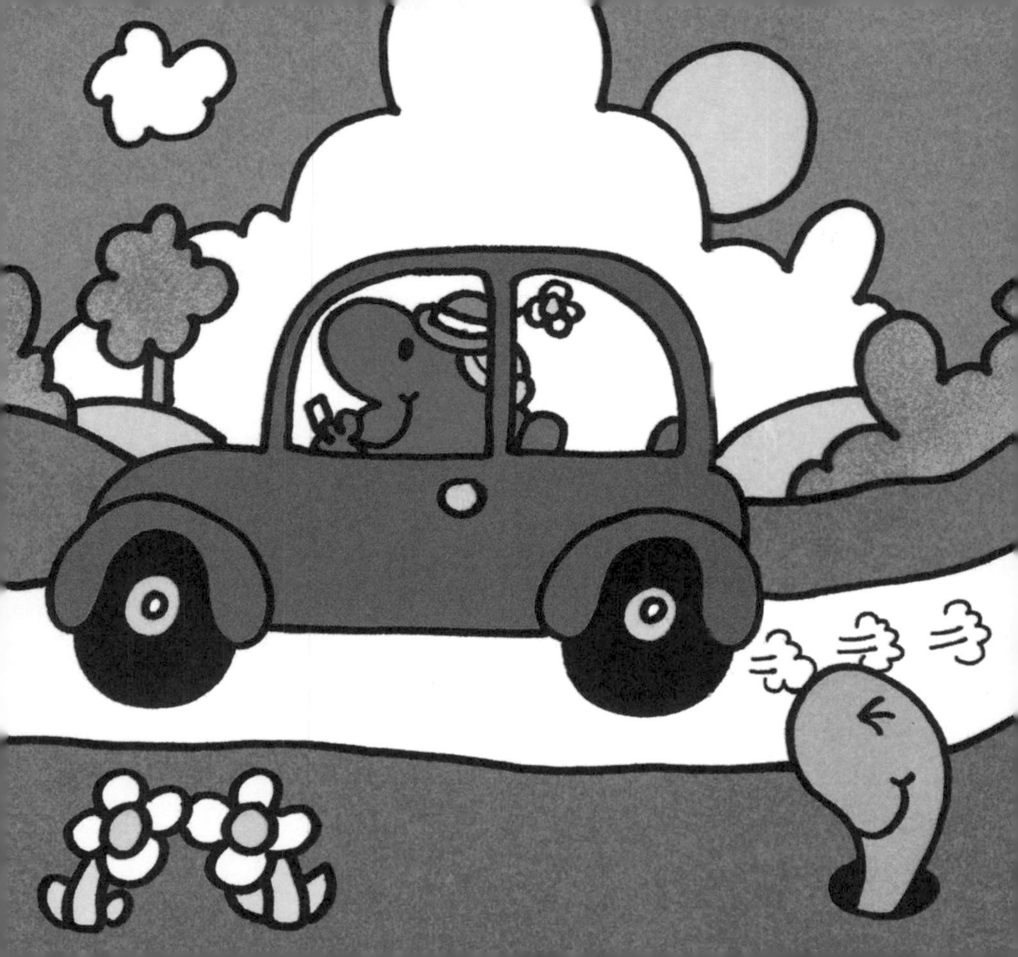

At 4 o'clock precisely, Little Miss Greedy pulled up in front of Mr Greedy's roly-poly sort of a house.

Mr Greedy was there to meet her.

"Hello, Little Miss Greedy," he smiled. "How lovely to see you after all this time!"

"Happy birthday," laughed Little Miss Greedy, and she gave Mr Greedy a big kiss.

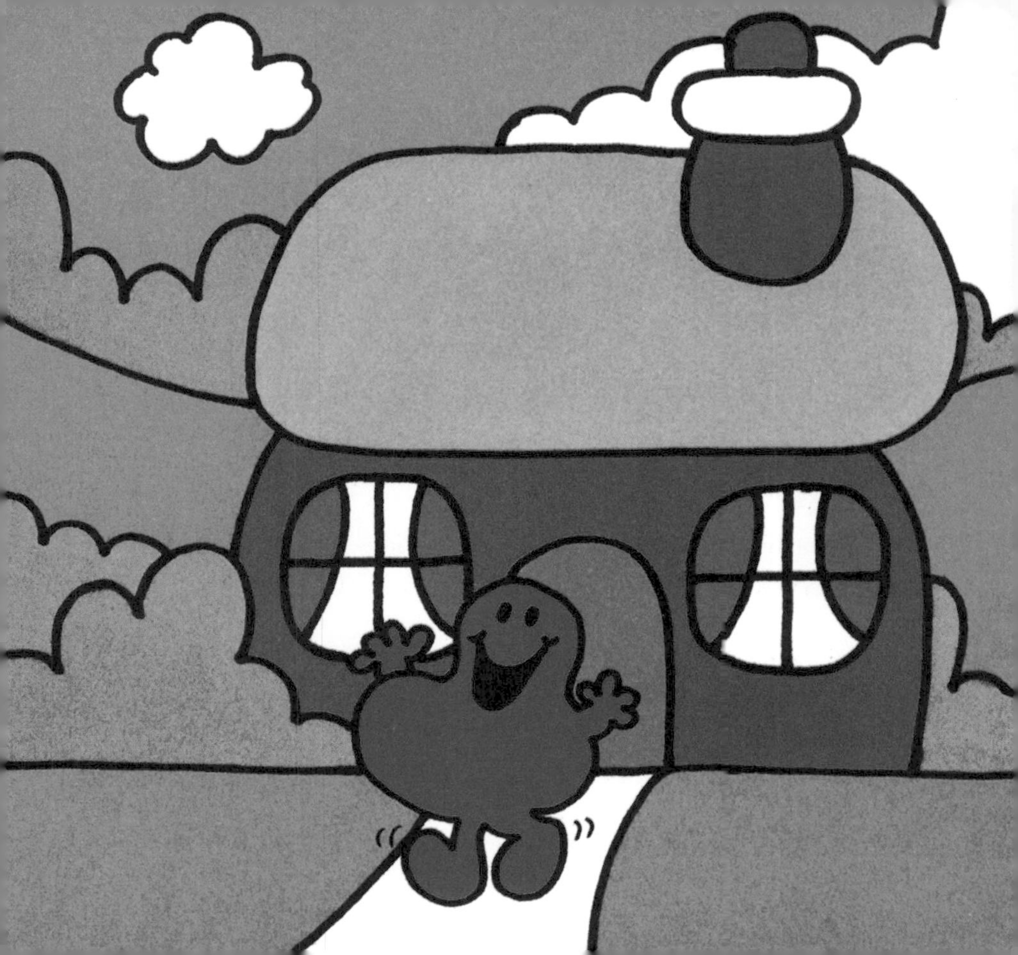

Mr Greedy blushed.

"Do come in," he said. "Tea's all ready!"

Little Miss Greedy was following Mr Greedy into
his house when she remembered something.
You know what it was, don't you?
That's right.
Mr Greedy's birthday present!

"Wait a minute," she said. "Can you help me to
lift something out of the back of my car, please?"
She smiled.
"It's rather heavy," she added.
"Certainly," agreed Mr Greedy.

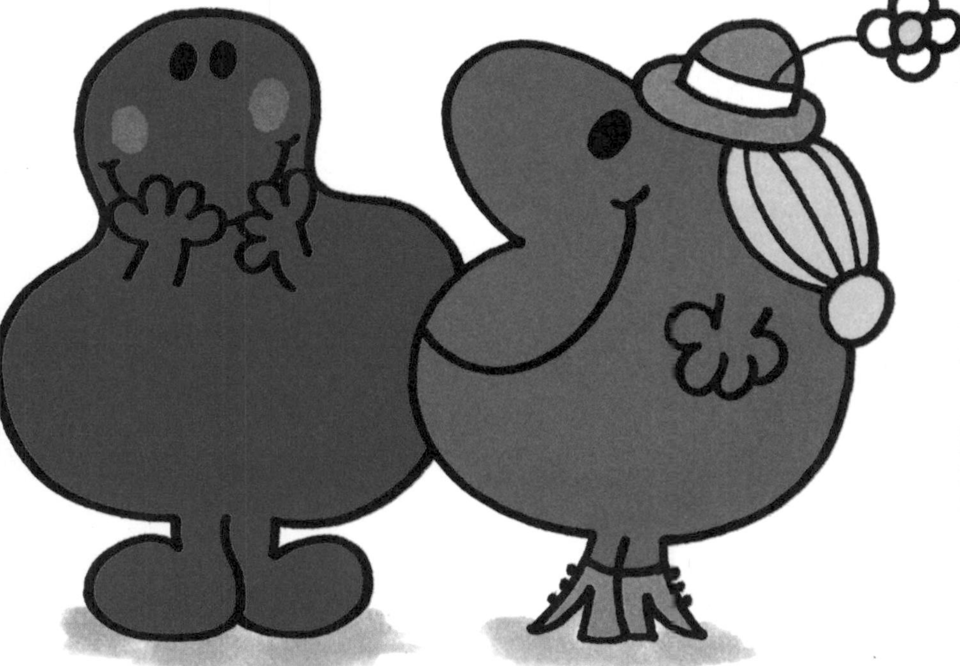

There, on the back seat of Little Miss Greedy's car, was the biggest birthday cake you've ever seen in all your life.

A huge, enormous, gigantic, colossal currant cake, with thick pink icing on top and strawberry jam in the middle.

"I only put one candle on it," explained Little Miss Greedy as they carried it to the house, "because I've forgotten how old you are!"

"Oh, you shouldn't have," laughed Mr Greedy. He licked his lips. "But I'm glad you did!"

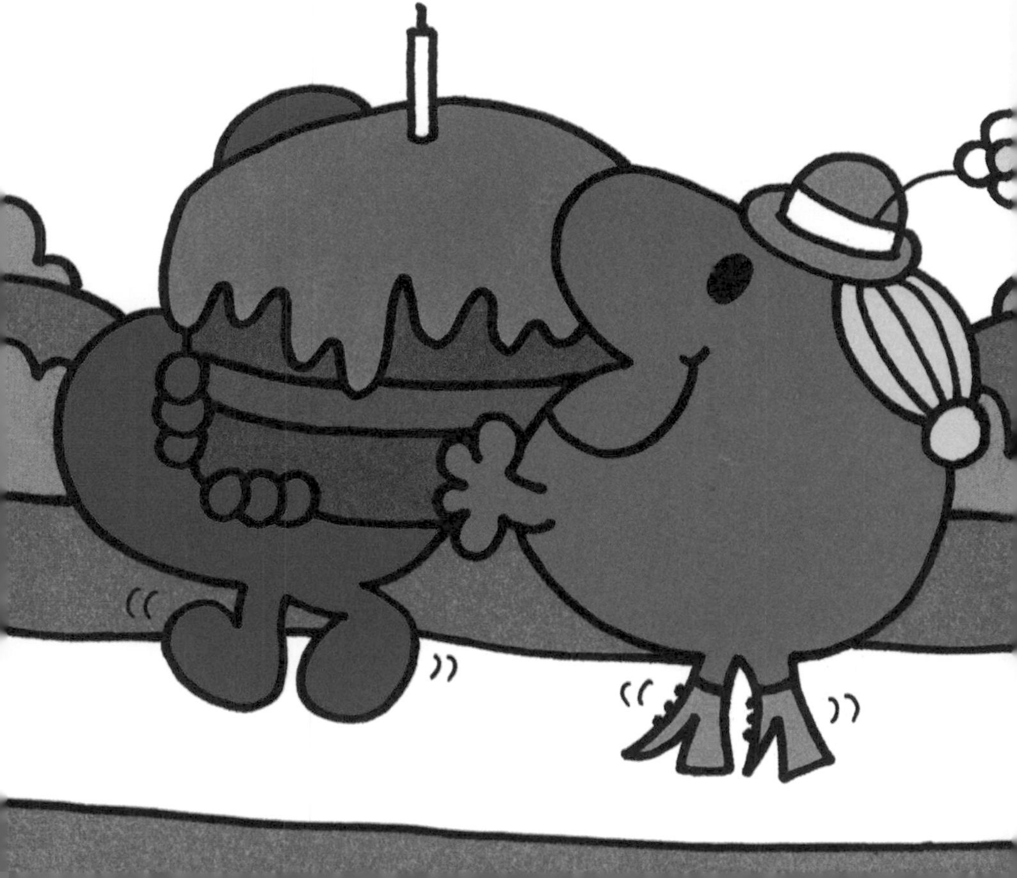

"I baked it today," said Little Miss Greedy.

And then she chuckled.

"I have a confession to make," she said.

"This isn't the only cake I baked today!
The first one looked so delicious,
I ate it for breakfast!"

She chuckled again.

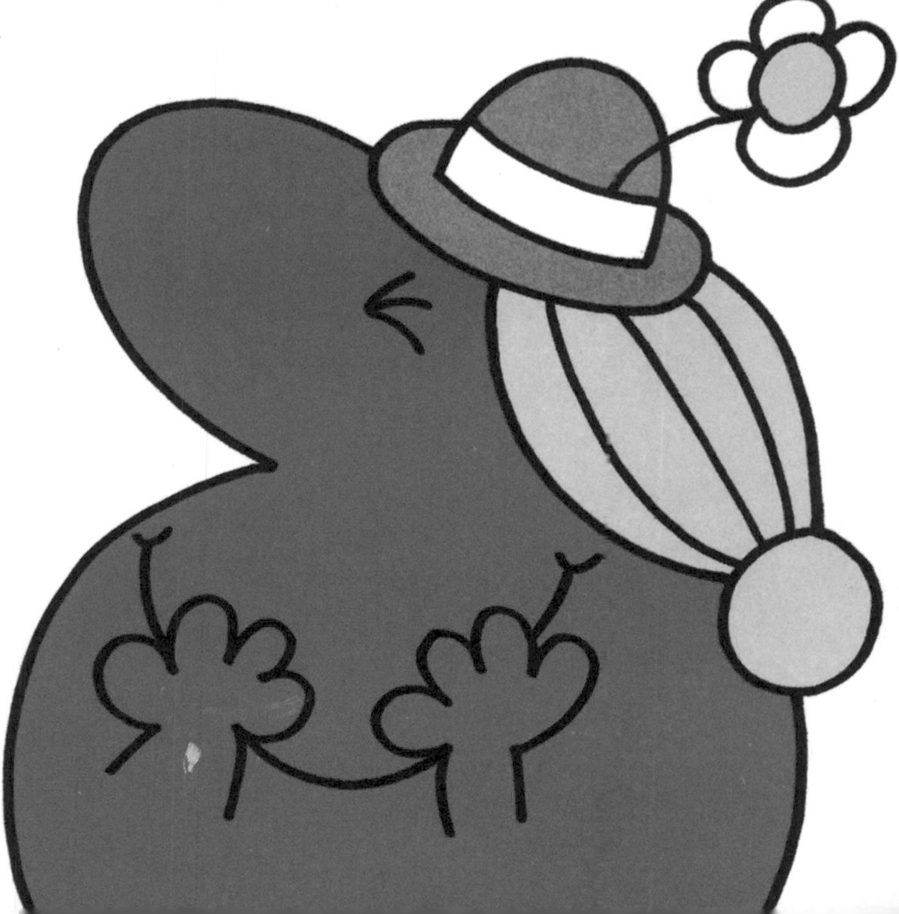

"And the second one looked so delicious,"
she went on,
"I ate that one for my lunch!"

Mr Greedy grinned from ear to ear.

"Time for tea, Little Miss Greedy" he said.

Fantastic offers for Little Miss fans!

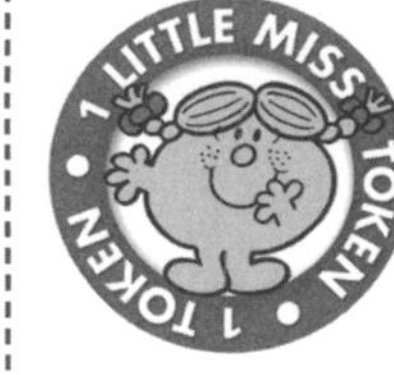
1 LITTLE MISS TOKEN
1 TOKEN

Collect all your Mr. Men or Little Miss books in these superb durable collectors' cases!
Only £5.99 inc. postage and packing, these wipe-clean, hard-wearing cases will give all your Mr. Men or Little Miss books a beautiful new home!

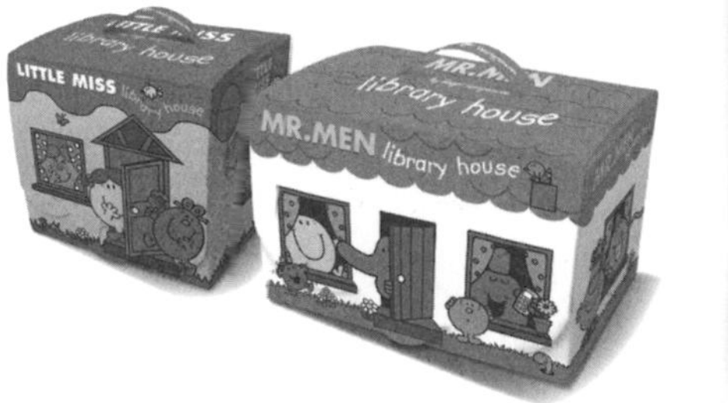
LITTLE MISS library house
MR.MEN library house

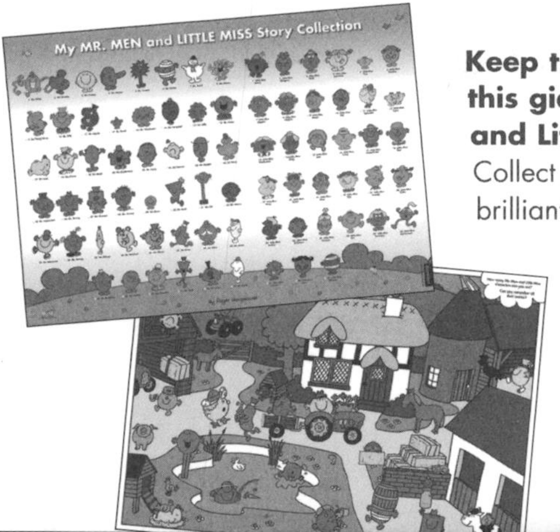
My MR. MEN and LITTLE MISS Story Collection

Keep track of your collection with this giant-sized double-sided Mr. Men and Little Miss Collectors' poster.
Collect 6 tokens and we will send you a brilliant giant-sized double-sided collectors' poster! Simply tape a £1 coin to cover postage and packaging in the space provided and fill out the form overleaf.

STICK £1 COIN HERE
(for poster only)

cut along the dotted line and return this whole page

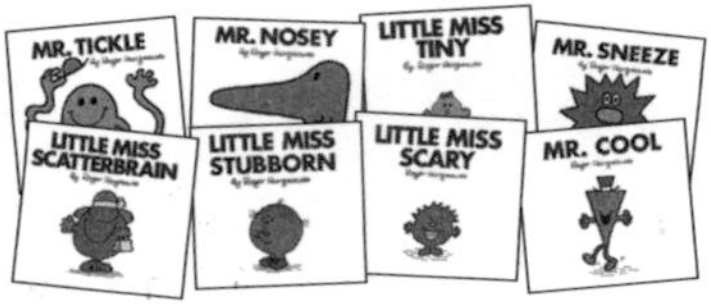
MR. TICKLE
MR. NOSEY
LITTLE MISS TINY
MR. SNEEZE
LITTLE MISS SCATTERBRAIN
LITTLE MISS STUBBORN
LITTLE MISS SCARY
MR. COOL

Only need a few Little Miss or Mr. Men to complete your set? You can order any of the titles on the back of the books from our Mr. Men order line on 0870 787 1724. Orders should be delivered between 5 and 7 working days.

TO BE COMPLETED BY AN ADULT

To apply for any of these great offers, ask an adult to complete the details below and send this whole page with the appropriate payment and tokens, to: MR. MEN CLASSIC OFFER, PO BOX 715, HORSHAM RH12 5WG

☐ Please send me a giant-sized double-sided collectors' poster.

AND ☐ I enclose 6 tokens and have taped a £1 coin to the other side of this page.

☐ Please send me ☐ Mr. Men Library case(s) and/or ☐ Little Miss library case(s) at £5.99 each inc P&P

☐ I enclose a cheque/postal order payable to Egmont UK Limited for £..................

OR ☐ Please debit my MasterCard / Visa / Maestro / Delta account (delete as appropriate) for £..................

Card no. ☐☐☐☐☐☐☐☐☐☐☐☐☐☐☐☐ Security code ☐☐☐

Issue no. (if available) ☐ Start Date ☐☐/☐☐/☐☐ Expiry Date ☐☐/☐☐/☐☐

Fan's name: .... Date of birth: ....

Address: ....

....

.... Postcode: ....

Name of parent / guardian: ....

Email for parent / guardian: ....

Signature of parent / guardian: ....

Please allow 28 days for delivery. Offer is only available while stocks last. We reserve the right to change the terms of this offer at any time and we offer a 14 day money back guarantee. This does not affect your statutory rights. Offers apply to UK only.

☐ We may occasionally wish to send you information about other Egmont children's books.
If you would rather we didn't, please tick this box.

Ref: LIM 001

cut along the dotted line and return this whole page